Praise for *Hap and Leonard: Blood and Lemonade*

"*Blood and Lemonade* is the best of Lansdale and the best of Hap and Leonard. As urgent as it is timeless. As fun as it is thoughtful. It haunts you while it kicks your ass. Joe never lets you down, just shows you over and over why he's the best."
—Jim Mickle, director of *Cold in July*

"A brilliant 'mosaic' novel. An amazingly vivid style that feels like Hemingway. Themes that are especially important for our time. With these early adventures of his compelling Hap and Leonard characters, Joe R. Lansdale hits a new high."
—David Morrell, *New York Times* bestselling author of *Murder as a Fine Art*

"Magnificent storytelling."
—*Char's Horror Corner*

"Joe Lansdale is our East Texas Hemingway, and here's another example of what makes him great. I*n Hap & Leonard: Blood and Lemonade,* he carves out beauty with plain words and direct sentences. Some of the stories in this mosaic novel are horrifying, others gritty, sad, thrilling, and funny, but all of them are beautiful. I ate it up."
—Daryl Gregory, author of *Spoonbenders* and *We Are All Completely Fine*

Praise for *Hap and Leonard*

"Seven laid-back adventures, one of them brand new, for "freelance troubleshooter" and good old boy Hap Collins and his gay black Republican partner Leonard Pine. . . . No one currently working the field demonstrates more convincingly and joyously the deep affinity between pulp fiction and the American tall tale."
—*Kirkus*

★ "Last seen in the novel *Honky Tonk Samurai*, Lansdale's incomparable East Texas crime fighting duo show their chops in this remarkable story collection. Readers can also look forward to the debut of the TV show *Hap and Leonard* on the Sundance Channel in March."
—*Publishers Weekly*, starred review

"An essential Hap and Leonard addition."
—*The Novel Pursuit*

". . . it's great to have all of these wonderful stories together in one nifty volume."
—*Horror Drive-In*

"A perfect introduction."
—*Booklist*

"East Texas charm, profane wit, and strong characterization, with enough snappy dialogue to keep a smile on your

face . . . excellent entertainment, edge-of-your-seat action one minute, gut-busting humor the next."
—*Adventures in Genre Fiction*

"This collection is crime/pulp fiction at its best and most captivating."
—*Risingshadow*

"If you find yourself on the wrong side of Hap and Leonard, be cautious, because they are quicker than a rattlesnake, and their bite is just as bad. If you find yourself an innocent bystander looking for a great book to read, you've come to the right place."
—*Killer Nashville*

"For those new to either Lansdale or the series, this latest collection is an excellent introduction to the kind of trouble these two often find themselves in; all the while exchanging some of the funniest, lovingly antagonistic, and memorial dialogue of any crime series."
—*Bookgasm*

Praise for Joe R. Lansdale's Hap and Leonard series

"Hap and Leonard function as a sort of Holmes and Watson—if Holmes and Watson had had more lusty appetites and less refined educations and spent their lives in East Texas. . . . Not only funny, but also slyly offers

acute commentary on matters of race, friendship and love in small-town America."
—*New York Times*

"Lansdale reveals the human condition—our darkest secrets and our proudest moments, all within the unlikely confines of an East Texas adventure featuring the two scruffiest protagonists in modern crime fiction."
—*Booklist*

"Hilarious. . . . Addictively scarfable. . . . Lansdale excels at dialogue, especially Hap and Leonard's lewd insult-a-thons. . . . Two thumbs-up, and pardon the barbecue smears."
—*Texas Monthly*

"Joe R. Lansdale is one of a kind. His Hap and Leonard novels should be read and treasured."
—James Swain, author of *Take Down*

"As usual, the dialogue is deadpan tart and the action extreme but convincing. . . . Lansdale once again proves he's the East Texas master of redneck noir."
—*Publishers Weekly* (on *Hyenas*)

Praise for Joe R. Lansdale

"Joe Lansdale is a born storyteller."
—Robert Bloch, author of *Psycho*

"There's no bullshit in a Joe Lansdale book. There's everything a good story needs, and nothing it doesn't."
—Christopher Moore, author of *Secondhand Souls*

"[Joe Lansdale has] a folklorist's eye for telling detail and a front-porch raconteur's sense of pace . . . a considerable literary intelligence at work."
—*New York Times Book Review*

"Joe Lansdale simply must be read."
—Robert Crais, author of the Elvis Cole and Joe Pike novels

"Read Joe Lansdale and see the true writer's gift."
—Andrew Vachss, author of *Shockwave*

"Among the best fiction writers in America today, Joe Lansdale turns on the juice and cuts the damn thing loose. Enjoy the ride!"
—Kinky Friedman, author of *Ten Little New Yorkers*

"Hunter S. Thompson meets Stephen King."
—Charles de Lint, author of *The Onion Girl*

"A master at taking a simple everyday event and turning reality upside down."
—*Mystery Scene*

Also by Joe R. Lansdale

Hap and Leonard mysteries

Savage Season (1990)
Mucho Mojo (1994)
The Two-Bear Mambo (1995)
Bad Chili (1997)
Rumble Tumble (1998)
Veil's Visit: A Taste of Hap and Leonard (1999)
Captains Outrageous (2001)
Vanilla Ride (2009)
Hyenas (2011)
Devil Red (2011)
Dead Aim (2013)
Honky Tonk Samurai (2016)
Hap and Leonard (2016)
Rusty Puppy (2017)

The Drive-In series

The Drive-In: A "B" Movie with Blood and Popcorn, Made in Texas (1988)
The Drive-In 2: Not Just One of Them Sequels (1989)
The Drive-In: A Double-Feature Omnibus (1997)
The Drive-In: The Bus Tour (2005)
The Complete Drive-In (2009, omnibus)

Ned the Seal

Zeppelins West (2001)
Flaming London (2005)
Flaming Zeppelins: The Adventures of Ned the Seal (2010)

Other novels

Act of Love (1981)
Texas Night Riders (1983, as Ray Slater)
Dead in the West (1986)
The Magic Wagon (1986)
The Nightrunners (1987)
Cold in July (1989)
Batman: Captured by the Engines (1991)
Tarzan: The Lost Adventure (1995, with Edgar Rice Burroughs)
The Boar (1998)
Freezer Burn (1999)
Waltz of Shadows (1999)
Something Lumber This Way Comes (1999)
The Big Blow (2000)
Blood Dance (2000)
The Bottoms (2000)
A Fine Dark Line (2002)
Sunset and Sawdust (2004)
Lost Echoes (2007)
Leather Maiden (2008)
All the Earth, Thrown to the Sky (2011)
The Ape Man's Brother (2012)
Edge of Dark Water (2012)
Hot in December (2013)
The Thicket (2013)
Black Hat Jack (2014)
Prisoner 489 (2014)
Paradise Sky (2015)
Fender Lizards (2015)

HAP AND LEONARD: BLOOD AND LEMONADE

JOE R. LANSDALE

HAP AND LEONARD

BLOOD AND LEMONADE

JOE R. LANSDALE

Interior and cover design by Elizabeth Story

Tachyon Publications LLC
1459 18th Street #139
San Francisco, CA 94107
415.285.5615
www.tachyonpublications.com
tachyon@tachyonpublications.com

Series Editor: Jacob Weisman
Editor: Richard Klaw

ISBN 13: 978-1-61696-253-1

Printed in the United States by Worzalla

First Edition: 2017
9 8 7 6 5 4 3 2 1

1.
PARABLE OF THE STICK

Leonard looked up from the newspaper he was reading, a little rag that was all that was left of our town paper, the bulk of it now being online, and glanced at me.

"So I'm reading in the paper here about how the high school, hell, grade school, all the grades, they got a no fighting policy, no matter who starts it. Some guy jumps you on the playground, lunch break, or some such, and you whack him in the nose so he'll leave you alone, you both go to detention."

"Can't have kids fighting. You and me, we fought too much. Maybe it's not a good thing to learn, all that fighting. We met at a fight, remember?"

"Horse shit," Leonard said, and put the paper down. "Look here, I know a thing about you, and I know how it was for me at school, with integration and all, and I don't think it works like that, and shouldn't. This whole thing about fighting to protect yourself, and getting the same punishment as the one who picks on you, how's that teaching common sense?"

"How's it work, Leonard?"

"Think on it. There's this thing I know about you, let's call it the parable of the stick."

I knew exactly what he was talking about.

I said, "Okay, let's call it that."

"You moved here from a smaller school, and I know you had some problems. We've talked about it. I wasn't there, but I know the drill. Try being black in a formerly all-white school sometime."

"I could try being black," I said, "but I'd still be white."

"You came to school from some little town to Marvel Creek. And there was this bully, a real asshole, bigger than you, and you were small then, right?"

"Not that I'm a behemoth now."

"No, you lack my manly physique, but you've grown into something solid. Then, though, you were a skinny little kid with hay fever and a plan to do something with your life. Which, of course, you failed to do. What were you going to be, by the way?"

"I don't know. A writer I thought."

"Ah, that's right. Hell, I knew that. It's been so long since you mentioned it, I forgot. Yeah, a writer. So you move here, a poor country kid with shabby clothes and his nose in a book, and this guy, this big kid, he picks on you. He does it every day. Calls you book worm or some such, maybe pencil dick. So what do you do? You do the right thing. You go to the principal and tell him the kid's fucking with you, and the principal says, okay, and he pulls the mean kid in and talks to him. So what's the mean little shit do the very next day?"

"Double beats the shit out of me."

"There you have it, but you're not fighting back, right?"

"Oh, I fought back. I just wasn't any good at it then. Probably why I learned martial arts."

"Sure it is. I did the same thing. I wasn't so little and didn't lose too much, but, like I said, I was a black kid in a formerly all-white school, and then there was my extraordinary beauty they were jealous of."

"Don't forget the massive dick."

"Oh yeah, the black anaconda that knows no friends. So this happens a few days in a row, this mean kid ignoring the principal, him not giving a greased dog turd what the principal said. You go home, and your dad, he sees you got a black eye and busted lip, and what does he do?"

"He tells me if he's bigger than me, bring him down to size."

"Right. He says, 'Hap, go out there and get yourself a good stick, 'cause there's plenty of them lying around on the edge of the playground by the woods. You get that big stick, and you lay for him, and when he don't expect it none, you bring that stick down on him so hard it will cause you to come up off the ground. Don't put his eye out with it, and don't hit him in the head, unless you have to, but use that stick with all your force, and if something breaks on him, well, it breaks. You get a licking every day and you don't do something back, taking that licking and being licked is gonna turn into a lifetime business.' He told you that, right?"

"Right."

"And you got you a stick next day at playground break, laid it up by the edge of the concrete wall on one side of the steps that led out of the school, and when the bell rang for the day to end, you got out there as quick as you could, ahead of the mean kid, and you picked up that stick."

"I did at that."

"And waited."

"Like a fucking hawk watching for a rat."

"Down the stairs he came, and you—"

"Swung that stick," I said. "Jesus. To this day I can still hear that fucking stick whistling in the wind, and I can still hear the way it met his leg just above the knee, right as he came down the last step. I remember even better that shit-eating, asshole-sucking grin he had on his face as he came down and saw me, before he realized about the stick. And better than that, I remember the way his face changed when he saw I had that stick. But it was too late for that motherfucker."

"What I'm saying."

"I caught him as he put his weight on his left leg. Smack of that stick on his hide was like a choir of angels had let out with one clean note, and down he went, right on his face."

"And when he started to get up?"

"I brought that stick down on his goddamn back with all I had in the tank, and oh my god, did that feel good. Then I couldn't stop, Leonard. I swear I couldn't."

"Tell it, brother. Tell it like it was. I never get tired of it."

"I started crying and swinging that stick, and I just couldn't fucking stop. Finally a teacher, a coach I think, he came out and got me and pulled me off that bastard, and that bastard was bawling like a baby and screaming, 'Don't hit me no more. Please don't hit me no more.' I actually started to feel bad about it, sorry for him—"

"As you always do," Leonard said.

"—and they carried me to the principal's office, and they brought the asshole in with me, and they put us in chairs beside one another, where we both sat crying, me mostly with happiness, and him because I had just beaten the living hell out of him with a stick and he had a fucking limp. He hurt so bad he could hardly walk."

"What did the principal do?"

"You know what he did."

"Yeah, but now that you're worked up and starting to sweat, let's not spoil it by you not getting it all out, 'cause I can tell right now, for you, the whole thing is as raw as if it happened yesterday."

"It is. The principal said, 'Hap, did you hit him with a stick?' and I say to him, 'Hard as I could.' The principal looks at the mean kid, says, 'And what did you do?' 'I didn't do nothing,' he says. 'No,' the principal said, 'what did you do the day before, and the day before that, and what were you told?' And the kid said, 'I was told to leave Hap alone.'"

"And what did the principal say?" Leonard said. "Keep on telling it."

"You're nuts, Leonard. You know what he said."

"Like I said, I never tire of hearing this one."

"He said to the kid, 'But you went back and did it again anyway, didn't you? You went back and did it because you wanted to pick on someone who you thought wouldn't fight back, or couldn't, but today, he was waiting for you. You didn't start it today, but you started it ever other day, and you got just what you deserve, you little bully. You picked on a nice kid that didn't want to fight and really just wanted to get along, and I know for a fact, he asked you to quit, and he came to me, and I came to you, and still you did it. Why?' 'I don't know,' he said. 'There you are,' said the principal, 'the mantra of the ignorant and the doomed.'"

I took a deep breath.

"I remember him saying just that. The ignorant and the doomed. Then the principal said to me, 'Hap. He picks on you again, you have my permission to pick up a stick and just whack the good ole horse hockey out of him. I catch you lying in wait for him again, or doing it because you can, then that's different. That makes you just like him, a low-life bully. He had this one coming, but he's only got it coming now if he starts it. But he picks on you, you give it to him back, and I won't do a thing. I won't say a word.'"

"There you have it," Leonard said. "That's the way we should have kept it. Self-defense is permissible."

"A stick was a little much," I said.

"Yeah, but these kids in school now, they're being taught to accept being victims. Why there's so many goddamn whiners, I think."

"That right?"

"You don't learn justice by taking it like the French. That's not how it works. Someone doesn't give you justice, you got to get your own."

"Or get out of the way of the problem."

"Alright, there's that. But then the motherfucker just moves down the road a little, and picks a new victim."

"I think you're trying to justify what we do sometimes."

"I don't need to justify it. Here's the thing, you get more shit from the meanies because the good folks don't stand up, don't know how, and don't learn how. And they're taught to just take it these days, and do it with a smile. Principal then, he knew what was up. You have any more trouble from the bully after that?"

"Not an inch worth," I said. "We became friends later, well, friendly enough. I think in his case it cured him across the board."

"So he didn't pick someone else to whip on?"

"No, but that doesn't mean it doesn't happen that way. I think he wasn't really a bad guy, just needed some adjustment, and I gave it to him. I think he had problems at home."

"Fuck him and his home," Leonard said. "Everyone now, they don't have an idea what's just, what's right, because they punish everyone the same. Ones that did it, and ones that didn't. I can see that if no one knows what went down, but now, even when they know who the culprit is, one who started it, it comes out the same for both. The good and the bad."

"Could have gone really bad. I could have killed that kid with that stick."

"That would have been too much, I guess," Leonard said.

"You guess?"

"Alright, maybe too much, but there's still something to learn there, still something your dad taught you that matters and has guided you ever since. Don't treat the just and righteous the same as the bad and the willfully evil, or you breed a tribe of victims and a tribe of evil bastards. Learning to be a coward is the same as learning to be brave. It takes practice. And that, my good brother, is the parable of the stick."

2.
TIRE FIRE

We went to the dojo where we trained and had a session in self-defense with the Shen Chuan instructor, and when that was over we had some free mat time. We sparred and did ground work and practiced throws until we were exhausted. We sat down on the mat with our backs against the wall, sweating and breathing hard. Everyone else had gone home, and since we had keys, we just sat there with the lights out and talked.

"Neither of us ever cross the line," Leonard said.

"I beg your pardon?" I said. "I think we have crossed a few lines."

"I mean in here, anywhere we train. We spar, and we go at it pretty hard, but we always hold back."

"We should. Someone might lose an eye."

"I mean we don't quite take the big step."

"That's because I don't hate you, Leonard. And, of course, I wouldn't want to embarrass you."

"It's like that, is it?"

"Pretty much . . . No, it's exactly like that."

"We could find out who's best, you know," Leonard said.

"There was that one time," I said.

"That was almost the real thing. I mean it hurt, and we came close to some damage, but we stalled most of it."

"I don't remember that much stalling," I said. "I thought you might be trying to prove something to yourself."

"Haven't you wondered which of us is the best?"

"Nope."

"Liar."

"I'll be honest," I said. "I don't want to find out."

"You got a point there," Leonard said.

"We might not like how we feel about one another afterwards."

"And your point sharpens."

"And, again, I wouldn't want to embarrass you."

"Oh, you are an asshole," Leonard said.

"You know, I will say this, first time I saw you, at that tire fire fight, I thought you were better than me then."

"Then and now," Leonard said.

"You're not going to give that up, are you? I've gotten a lot better."

"Yeah, but you're lazy. I train harder."

"Probably," I said. "That night, I think you might

could have whipped anyone in the world, and I include one of my heroes, Muhammad Ali."

"Greatest fucking boxer that ever lived."

"But he was a boxer. We cheat a lot more. Boxing, maybe he does get you, but the whole enchilada, not so much."

"Kick, bite, head-butt, lock, throw, do ground work, and pick up a stick if it's available," Leonard said.

"What I'm saying."

"It was a hell of a night."

"You know that's right."

It was a night hunt, and I was sick of the whole thing already. I didn't want to shoot any coons or possums, or much of anything. I was ready to get home and shower and pick the ticks off my balls. Sure, coon can be eaten, and I knew families who did, mostly black families, but I didn't want none of it, and unlike my uncle, I didn't sell the skins.

A lot of people ate possum, our family included, if there was nothing else. To me it tasted like greasy pork, and the best way to eat possum was catch it and put it up and feed it some corn for a week or two, and then kill and eat it. But I didn't like to do that anymore, on account of I got attached to the damn things. I was still sick over the hogs we had butchered. I had got to know them. There was a thing Winston Churchill said in a book I read, about how dogs looked up to you, cats down on you, but hogs treated you as equals. This was true, and on that account I was through butchering hogs myself, and from then on my parents, to placate me, bought our pork chops and bacon wrapped in cellophane and found in the freezer section at the store. I preferred being a hypocrite, eating meat someone else killed.

It was finding an animal in a trap that was still alive, seeing my uncle dispatch it with a shotgun butt, that had put me off the idea of trapping and hunting, that and me shooting a bird for no good reason other than to see it fall, and finding it lying on the ground, its beak open, trying desperately to draw in air, its eyes glazing over like a sugar donut. It got to me. One dead bird and thousands of bird songs unsung for no goddamn good reason other than I wanted to see a bird fall.

So there we were out in the woods at night, and I was thinking this was my last hunt, though it wouldn't be, but it would be for a long while. There was a can of Wolf Brand Chili at home, and that was good enough for me. Me and Roger had been hunting and fishing together for years, and on this night we had gone into the woods to spotlight critters, shoot them out of trees, bag them and take them home to be dressed and cooked, but as I said, I knew that night I had completely lost my interest in hunting unless I was actually hungry. Girls were far more interesting. Some of the boys called chasing girls hunting squirrel, which came from the idea that their pubic hair was a pelt. It wasn't exactly forward thinking, but there you have it. Everything in East Texas was compared to hunting.

Our trek had brought us down by the riverside, using our headband lights to travel by. Down close to the river I could smell fish, and then a smell that took me a moment to figure out. It was burning rubber.

We could see the fire after a moment, and it was pretty big. There was an old abandoned, tumbling-down sawmill on the other side of the river where the fire was, and there was a clearing in front of the mill, and it wasn't unusual for kids to drive down there to smoke dope, drink and screw, throw rocks in the water and fire off guns.

The fire was really big, and we could see the silhouettes of people cast off by the firelight. Two of the shadows were moving quickly, and the rest were still, forming what looked like a dark tree line, or the craggy shapes of a mountain. We could hear voices too, some of them yelling. As we neared, moving along the tree line on our side, the voices rose up and rolled over the river like a tide, and came to us in excited cries and yells. There was the sound of grunting, and a slapping sound, as if someone were beating a car seat from time to time with a belt.

Finally we could see the people making the shadows, but we couldn't figure out who was who or what was what. We turned off our headlamps and took them off our heads, and from what I could tell it didn't matter. No one had noticed us when our lights were on.

Roger said, "You want to go see what's happening?"

I didn't, but I was seventeen and didn't want Roger to think my balls hadn't dropped, so I said, "Yeah, let's go see."

We had to go down a pretty good distance before we came to the Swinging Bridge. It was a bridge that had been put across the river by some oil company so they could get down there and drill for oil. It had been built back in the thirties during the oil boom that had engulfed that region. Whole towns had been created by the oil boom overnight. The oil was pulled up and out, and then it was gone, and so was the bulk of the towns. Some survived, like Marvel Creek, made up of a handful of folks rich from the oil boom, and about three or four thousand others, oil field trash, whores, white trash, and poor blacks, a few you might call middle class.

Roger and I went over the bridge, but when we were about halfway over, Roger caught my arm, said, "I changed my mind. I don't want to see what's over there. I can see enough already. Lots of white boys down there, and in case you haven't noticed, I'm black."

"Hard to miss that," I said.

Where we were on the bridge it was dark, and there were trees that ran alongside the river, and there was a gap in them. Through the gap we could see a heap of tires stacked on top of one another, all of them set ablaze, most likely by a nice coating of gasoline and a tossed match. In the light of the fire two young men were fighting. There were two other men lying on the ground. The others were standing or sitting on a rise above them, watching. There was no one along the river's edge, and the firelight licked out and sent burnt orange light against the shoreline and fell into the water and wavered with its movement. The fighters' shadows hopped about.

"It's a money fight," Roger said.

I knew about them. I had been told I ought to fight in them myself, as I was good with my hands and feet and the money was alright. You could also get bad hurt. Some of the folks involved were school kids, but the fighters came from all around, and could range from eighteen to thirty. It was said a young man from over Mineola had been killed somewhere out here, and that his body had been dumped in the river.

I don't know if it was true or not, probably not, but it was a story that went around like the flu. I knew a lot of the kids in the group, and I knew one of the fighters, the white guy, Charlie. He was an asshole and a bully at school. We had words now and again, but hadn't exchanged blows; it was close a few times. I knew I was tough, but he scared me a little. He carried a knife and had pulled it at school a couple times.

The young man he was fighting was black. Firelight flickered over his skin like a fevered tongue licking chocolate. He moved smooth and quick, up on his toes, his right side forward, his right hand flicking out and jabbing Charlie as fast as a hungry chicken pecking corn.

Roger said, "I ain't going down there after all. There's enough white boys down there to make a surfing movie, and them white girls being there too, they're bound to show out, and they might show out on me. I can't believe that nigger is down there. What the fuck?"

"He's got balls, alright," I said.

"What he ain't got is brains," Roger said. "I do. I don't want to go down there."

"I'm going over," I said. "You got to go on, go. I won't hold it against you."

"Hap, them other boys, they don't see things like you. They haven't been listening to Dr. King on the TV. They ain't never read *Uncle Tom's Cabin*."

"That book's a slow go, by the way," I said. "But you know what, Roger?"

"What?'

"You got a rifle and I got a shotgun."

"Nothing says they ain't got cannons of their own."

"I hear you," I said. "Go on back you want. Wait for me up by the truck."

"It'll take me two hours or so to get back, and then I got to wait on you?"

"Then wait on the bridge for me."

"Damn, Hap. I can't let you go down there by yourself."

"Yeah you can."

"Shit, but I ain't. Goddamn me."

We crossed the bridge and went walking along the riverbank, toward the fighters, past where all their cars were parked. We came first to the two white guys, shirtless, laying out on the ground near the river unconscious. When the fire flicked just right I could see how badly their faces were bruised and cut up. The black fighter was still moving catlike, and Charlie was taking his beating like he was tied to a post. When Charlie moved at all, he dragged one leg behind him as if it was in a bucket full of concrete. If he'd ever had any spring in his step it was well sprung.

The black fighter was smiling, and I thought I could hear him laughing, a kind of deep gurgle that came up from his chest. When we got closer I saw that Charlie's face looked as if someone had been to work on it with a razor. It was cut and bleeding all over.

"Call me a nigger again, you shit-cracker. Go on, call me one."

Charlie wasn't saying anything, and in fact, he seemed to have trouble breathing. But I had a good idea that the word "nigger" had left his mouth earlier during the fight. It had come out of Roger's mouth too, but that was different. Roger owned it, but people like Charlie used it like a knife. It was like poor folks calling themselves white trash. It was alright for them to say it, but unless you wanted to wake up in a ditch with a fence post up your ass, might be best you didn't call them that unless you were meaner or had a bigger gun.

Finally Charlie went down on one knee and held out a hand, palm forward.

The black fighter quit dancing, smiled with blood-coated teeth.

"Get up, peckerwood. I'm not through with you. Get up and let me knock some of those teeth down your throat. Come on, man. Call me nigger again."

I saw then that Charlie's buddy Kilgore, another of my least favorite people, was coming down the slight rise toward them, carrying an axe handle in his hand. Three other big boys came down from the crowd then, and a kind of cheer went up from the folks gathered there, as if lions had just been released into the arena. I heard Kilgore say, "I'm gonna sort you out, nigger."

"Bring it," said the black fighter. "And I hope you brought a sack lunch, motherfucker, 'cause you're gonna be here all night."

I checked the two guys knocked out and on the ground, to see how things with them were. Same as before. I hadn't seen either of them move a muscle since I came up. For all I knew they were dead.

I walked over then, and the black fighter wheeled toward me, saw that I had a shotgun. There was only a moment of hesitation, and then he gave me a look like: Go on and shoot me, and watch the goddamn buckshot bounce off.

I yelled out to the boys coming down the hill.

"This looked to be a fair fight to me. You fuckers ought to go on back up the hill and put your hands back up the dresses of the whores you came with."

"Hey," I heard one of the girls say.

I saw it was a girl I knew. I said, "Sorry. Juliet. I'm assuming you're an independent."

Kilgore said, "Hap Collins, you cocksucker. You taking up for a nigger?"

I said to the fighter, "You a nigger?"

"In some circles," he said. "But I like to think of myself as well-tanned."

"In the circles that count," I said loud enough the crowd of about twenty could hear me, "this fellow thinks of himself as well-tanned."

"Oh fuck you," Kilgore said.

"Nigger lover," someone in the group yelled down.

"Told you," Roger said.

I walked around on the other side of the black fighter and looked up the rise at Kilgore, the crowd behind him, the old, tumbling-down saw mill behind all of them.

I said, "Why don't you come down and see if you can spread my legs for that fucking."

Kilgore didn't move, and the others with him had sort of drifted off to the sides, like maybe they just realized they had left something in their cars that they badly needed.

"You're a big man with a fucking shotgun," Kilgore said.

"Yeah," I said. "What if I let Roger here hold it, and then you and me step up to the plate and see who's the best batter?"

"Nothing would please me more. I'd take great pleasure in that, Collins."

"He's pretty big," the black fighter said, and grinned at me. I could see me and him were about the same age.

"He is, isn't he?" I said.

"Yeah, he is," Roger said.

"If I lose, Roger, you can shoot him with your rifle."

"Oh, nice," Roger said. "Be a nigger lynching come morning. If it takes that long."

"Give me your shotgun," said the black fighter. "I'll hold it for you."

I gave it to him without hesitation and he held it cradled in his arms. He was comfortable with it. I had an idea he knew how to use it quite well.

I took off my shirt and threw it on the ground and stepped up where the two had been fighting. Charlie had half-crawled, half-stumbled off, and fell down not too far from the tire fire, near the other two. The black fighter was starting a collection.

Kilgore tossed the axe handle aside, and started pulling his tee-shirt over his head. He came down and stood across from me and smiled. He figured it was going to be easy. I figured he might be right. I have been known to shoot off my mouth and regret it later.

"I know you're gonna take him, white boy," the black fighter said. "I know you will."

I didn't say it aloud, but I thought: That makes one of us.

Roger gave me a bit of advice. "Keep your left up, Hap."

"Thanks," I said. But like the black fighter, I fought power side out. I had learned that from my dad, who not only taught me boxing and wrestling fundamentals, but had taught me some self-defense. The rest of what I had learned so far came from the judo and hapkido I had learned at the Tyler, Texas YMCA.

"You ain't got to fight him for me," the black fighter said. "I just wanted to see you'd do it or not. I can whip him same as the others."

"You've fought three," I said. "I think it's only fair you have a little break between."

"That's awfully white of you . . . What is it? Happy?"

"Hap," I said. "Hap Collins. My friends just call me He Who Has A Massive Dick."

He laughed a little, then said, "I'm Leonard. Leonard Pine."

"Shut up, you fuckers" said Kilgore. "Let's get on with it."

"He's crowing for you to give him his ass beating," Leonard said.

I was glad Leonard was confident.

Leonard moved back and Kilgore moved down, and the crowd above eased down closer, and I saw that one of the boys who had walked away earlier was walking back with a revolver. Leonard yelled up at him, "Put that on the ground right now, or I shoot your kneecap off and piss down your throat. I mean it, motherfucker."

Leonard lifted the shotgun. I feared he might mean it.

The fellow bent over and gently laid the gun down.

Leonard said, "Now walk away, chief."

Chief walked away. He joined the others and sat at the top of the rise and looked embarrassed.

Me and Kilgore started to move then. And there was something I couldn't explain. Something in me that was always there, a kind of fire, a burning anger, the source of which I had no idea. It was always there in the background, and though I didn't hunt because I didn't want to kill, the primal urge was there, but it had shifted from animals to bullies and assholes and no goods. I could feel that anger warming my muscles.

Kilgore said, "I'm going to kick your ass, and then you, nigger, you're next. I'm gonna knock the black off of you."

Leonard pointed at himself. "Okay, which nigger? Me or the other one?"

"I put Collins down, then it's you two darkies. One at a time, or both together. Count on it."

Leonard laughed. "Shit, you couldn't roll me over if I was dead, let alone whip my ass."

Roger didn't say anything. He just held tight to his rifle.

Me and Kilgore moved in a circle, and then we moved together, and then Kilgore threw a haymaker from the pits of hell. It brought with it fire and brimstone and lots of power, but it was slow. It was like watching a big truck with no gas being pushed up hill by weak men with hernias.

I leaned back. The punch passed. I stepped in and made a short, front right-handed hook to the side of his jaw. I heard a terrible sound that made me wince. I knew it was bone cracking. Kilgore went down in the dirt and the dirt flew up and made a little cloud that drifted quickly back to earth.

Kilgore didn't get up.

"Son-of-a-bitch," Leonard said. "You are the man, goddamnit."

"Took me a little longer than I anticipated," I said. "But I been sick."

Leonard laughed out loud. "You are something, white boy, something."

"I know," I said, trying not to show how surprised I was that I had been so successful so quickly. My hand hurt though.

"Anyone else want some of my boy here?" Leonard yelled up. "Anyone. I got money. I'll lay that money out right now."

No one wanted any of his boy.

Leonard said, "Alright then. I'm gonna expect all the debts to be paid up. I put down three of your fuckers, and you put down none of me."

"I forgot to bet on myself," I said.

"You did," Roger said. "You just hurt your knuckles for nothing."

I sucked on the blood across my knuckles.

"Shit, it was worth it," I said.

Leonard had gone up the hill with my shotgun to collect the bets. He stopped and picked up the revolver that had been dropped and brought it back with him and tossed it in the Sabine.

"Shit, man," said the boy who had dropped it. "That's my old man's."

"He gets it back," Leonard said, "he's gonna have to be Aquaman."

"Now everybody go home," I said. "Oh, and come down here and get your guys, or we'll dump them in the river."

A few of the guys came down and picked up the two Leonard had knocked out, and one guy helped Charlie stagger up the hill. I looked over at Kilgore. Leonard was standing over him pissing in his face.

"The white don't wash off," Leonard said.

"You know it don't," I heard Roger say.

"That's a surprise to me," Leonard said. "I always thought it was paint."

In a few minutes the fighters were loaded up, including piss-face Kilgore, and at the top of the hill, the guy whose gun Leonard had thrown in the water said, "I'll get you at school, Collins."

"Sure. Meet you on the playground."

He went over to his car and got inside with a girl, drove away, following a procession of cars, on up and out of the bottoms.

Leonard came over and stuck out his hand. I shook it.

"That was some punch," he said. "Took me longer with these guys."

"I watched you move," I said. "You did alright. Hell, you put down three."

"I did, didn't I?"

"I held my rifle and looked confident," Roger said.

"You did indeed." I said.

"That white boy threatened you," Roger said. "That's Robbie Wayne. He's supposed to be bad."

"He didn't offer to fight," I said. "He's not so bad. He could have had his moment now, but he decided to save it for later. He's a blow hard. He won't bother me."

"I wasn't worried about you," Roger said. "I was thinking about me."

"Shit. Call on Hap here, he'll hit so hard he won't wake up until next July. You know you broke that boy's jaw, don't you?"

"I hope so," I said.

"Man," Leonard said. "You're alright."

"Thanks," I said, buttoning up my shirt.

Leonard gave me my shotgun. He said, "Hey, take some of this money I won. You ought to."

"I don't want it," I said. "You keep it."

"They have fights here regularly," Leonard said. "I had a bunch of black guys coming, but they all faded out at the last minute. I should have gone home, I guess. But I sure wanted to hit somebody. You know the Klan used to whip blacks out here in front of the saw mill? I heard they hung one or two out here by the river. Guy named Mose for one, but there might have been others."

"I've heard that," I said.

"I got my car hid back a piece, off a little road," Leonard said. "I was afraid what they might do to it after I knocked them around."

"Confident, aren't you?" Roger said.

"Hell, yeah," Leonard said. "So long you two. And a special so long to you, Hap Collins. I hope we cross paths again."

"It could happen," I said.

Leonard started up and over the rise. He didn't show any sign of exhaustion. Way he moved you would have thought he'd just gotten out of bed after a long night's good rest.

"He was a cat, wasn't he?" Roger said.

"I'll say," I said.

"You two seem a lot alike."

"I know," I said. "I knew that right off."

I looked to see where Leonard was going. He walked along the edge of the saw mill and melted into the woods.

3.
NOT OUR KIND

We got up and turned on the lights and sparred a little more, but we were pretty worn by then, so we didn't last long.

"Want to get an ice cream cone?" I said. "We could go through the drive through at Dairy Queen."

"You and the goddamn ice cream," Leonard said. "You could drop a few pounds, you know?"

"I could also enjoy a very nice chocolate cone, and you, a vanilla."

"Damn," Leonard said. "Vanilla is my kryptonite. They made vanilla pussy I could quit being queer."

"No you couldn't."

We locked up and I drove us to Dairy Queen. It was full dark now and there were quite a few cars on the LaBorde streets. More than usual, I thought, but the ebb and flow of traffic in a small city, or a big town, is sometimes hard to figure. I was beginning to think it was getting too big for me. Everywhere you looked there were people. Our house was on a nice lot, but there were still close neighbors and the traffic on our division street had increased of late. Brett and I had talked about it, but the house we had now we had almost paid off and the idea of moving was a chore.

Leonard said, "I remember when us just being together, a black guy and white guy in East Texas, was a big deal."

"Yeah, everyone would do a double take."

"I used to see black and white couples together, I'd do a double take," Leonard said. "It was so unusual then."

"Especially if there appeared to be anything romantic about it."

"Yeah, interracial couples didn't show up in public much," Leonard said. "Mostly because they didn't want to get their asses beat, or maybe even killed."

"Sometimes I think things are bad, and then I realize how much progress has been made."

"Not enough."

"Nope," I said. "Not enough."

"I'll say this for you, Hap. You hung with me back then, and me being queer didn't help either."

"Gay, Leonard. Gay. That's the term. You see, queer is for the homophobes."

"Gay, queer, bent, what have you," he said. "Besides, we people, as some refer to us, often use the word too. We've claimed it. Can I say nigger?"

"I hate you," I said.

Leonard snickered.

"We are going to need to have you go see someone about how to talk in the modern world," I said.

"Too much bullshit as it is," Leonard said.

"Can't fault that sentiment."

As we pulled up to the drive-through, Leonard said, "Hey, let's go inside. I'd like a burger before that cone."

"Talk about me," I said.

"Yeah, but I'm not fat."

We parked at the Dairy Queen, went inside. We ordered and went to the back and sat at a booth. It was an oddly empty place considering all the traffic, just me and Leonard and the staff.

"You know," I said. "One time I was sitting in the back of another Dairy Queen, one in Marvel Creek, and some fellows came to talk to me about you, and they didn't have anything nice to say about you."

"Few do . . . Oh, wait. That was around the time you and me had our first showdown with someone. Together, I mean."

"That would be it."

When I got out of school that day, I drove over to the Dairy Queen to get a hamburger before I had to go to work at the aluminum chair plant. I had a work permit, so I got off early, and I usually grabbed a burger, and then I drove out to the plant and worked until midnight. A lot of us from high school worked there, making fifty-six dollars and fourteen cents a week, which wasn't even good for 1968.

I was sitting at the back of the Dairy Queen, eating quickly, and was about halfway through the burger when four boys from school came in. I knew one of them pretty well, and the others a little. We all knew each other's names, anyway. I can't say any of them were friends of mine. We ran in different circles.

They saw me and came over. Two of them sat down in my booth, across from me, and the other two sat out to the side at a table and leaned on their elbows and looked at me. I didn't like their attitude.

"What's going on?" I said.

"You're seeing it," the one I knew best said. His name was David. Last time I saw him was at the Swinging Bridge, where I met Leonard. Me and him hit it off.

We saw each other again in Marvel Creek, running into one another accidentally at first, and then finally on purpose. He lived over in LaBorde with his uncle, but they came to the general store in Marvel Creek to shop, which I didn't understand. Everyone in Marvel Creek goes to the larger city of LaBorde to shop, but his uncle had a store in Marvel Creek he liked, place where he had been buying shoes for a long time. He liked it, Leonard said, because the owner never told him to come around back, even before laws were passed that said he didn't have to.

David said, "We were talking about you the other day."

"Were you?" I said.

"Yeah. Some. We been seeing you around with that nigger."

"Leonard?"

"One name is as good as another for a nigger. 'Boy' will work. We'll call him 'Boy.'"

"I won't. And if I was you, I wouldn't call him that. You might find yourself turned inside out and made into a change purse."

"You think he's tough, don't you?"

"Don't you? You seen him whip some ass at the Swinging Bridge, same as me."

"We seen you whip some too," another of the boys said, "but that don't scare us none, about you or the nigger."

The big guy's real name was Colbert, but everyone called him Dinosaur on account of he was big and not that smart. He was a football player and he thought he was as cool as an igloo. He was said to be the toughest guy in school. That might have been true. He hadn't been at the bridge that night. I didn't know if he'd seen me and Leonard together or not, but he was riled about it, thanks to David.

I didn't like where this was going. I kept eating, but I didn't taste the rest of the burger.

"Way we see it," David said, and bobbed his head a little so as to indicate the others, "you aren't doing yourself any good."

"Oh, how's that?"

"Ought not have to spell it out for you, Hap. Hell, you know. Hanging with a nigger."

"You mean Leonard."

"Yeah. Okay. Leonard the nigger."

I nodded. I didn't realize until that moment that I really liked Leonard, and these guys I had known all my life, if only a little, I didn't care for that much at all.

"Word's getting around you're a nigger-lover," Dinosaur said.

"Is it?"

"Yeah. You don't want that," David said.

"I don't?"

"Are you trying to be a smartass?" Dinosaur said.

"I don't think so," I said. I put one foot out of the booth so I could move if I had to, could get a position to fight or run.

"There's talk, and it could reflect on you," David said.

"In what way?"

"You think girls want to date a nigger-lover? And way we hear it, this guy's queer as a three-dollar bill, and proud of it. A nigger queer, come on, man. You got to be kidding me."

"But he has such a nice personality," I said.

"You aren't going to listen, are you?" David said. "Girls don't want to date no nigger-lover."

"You said that."

"Because it's true."

"So, you have come here to spare me being viewed in

a bad way, and to make sure I don't lose my pussy quota? That's what's up?"

"You're making light of something you shouldn't," David said. "We got a way of doing things, and you know it."

"We got to keep it protected," Dinosaur said.

"We?" I said.

"White people," David said. "Now that niggers can vote and eat with us, they think they can act like us."

I nodded, glanced at the two that hadn't spoken. "You guys, you thinking the same?"

They all nodded.

"Civil rights may change how the Yankees live," David said, "but it won't change us."

"That's why I don't like you guys."

This landed on their heads like a rock.

"You don't have to like us, but we can't have one of our own hanging about with niggers. He's not our kind. He's not one of us."

"You know, it's really been nice, but I have to go to work now, so I'll see you."

I got up and eased past Dinosaur, keeping an eye on him, but trying to look like I wasn't concerned.

They all stood up. I was about halfway to the door when they came up behind me. David grabbed at my arm. I popped it free.

"You better take in what we're saying," David said.

"I could throw you through that window glass right now," Dinosaur said.

"You might need yourself a nap and a sack lunch before you're able to throw me through that glass, or anywhere else for that matter," I said.

I was bluffing. I was a badass, and I knew it. But four guys, badass or not, are four guys. And one of them was a fucking freak of nature. I was reminded of how freakish he was with him standing almost as close to me as a coat of paint. He was looking down at me with a head like a bowling ball, shoulders wide enough to set a refrigerator on one side, a stove on the other.

About that time, the manager, Bob, came out from behind the counter. An older guy, red-haired, slightly gone to fat, not as big as Dinosaur, but I'd seen him throw out a couple of oil workers once for throwing ketchup-soaked fries against the Dairy Queen glass to see who could make theirs stick and not slide off. They didn't get very far in that game.

What I remember best was one of those guys, after Bob had tossed them out like they were dirty laundry, pulled a knife and held it on Bob when he came outside to make sure they were leaving.

Bob laughed, said to that guy, "Should have brought yourself a peppermint stick, you oil field trash. They're a hell of a lot easier to eat."

This with the tip of the knife pressed to his stomach. The guy with the knife and his buddy believed Bob. Believed him sincerely. They were out of there so fast they practically left a vapor trail. It seemed they were standing there outside the Dairy Queen one moment, and the next their car's taillights were shining red in the distant night.

Bob said to David and the others, "Alright, boys. Take it outside."

I thought, shit. Outside isn't going to be all that better for me.

We all started outside. Even Dinosaur didn't want a piece of Bob.

As we were going, Bob put his hand on my shoulder. "You stay with me."

The others turned and looked at Bob. "Unless I've developed a stutter, you know what I said."

They hesitated about as long as it takes to blink, and went out.

Bob waited until they were outside and looking through the glass. He made a shooing movement with his hand, and they went away. After a moment I saw their car drive by the window and on out to the highway.

"They'll be watching for you, son."

"I know."

"Hanging with niggers is frowned on. I got some nigger friends, but you got to know how to keep them at a distance. I go fishing with a couple of them, but I don't have them around at my house, sitting in my chairs and eating at my table."

"Thanks," I said. "I'll remember that."

"Still, no cause to pick on someone. You or the nigger. They don't get to choose to be niggers. And you can get along with most anyone, and learn from most anyone, even a nigger. I learned how to catch catfish good from one."

Well, Bob was better than the other four.

I bought a bag of chips and a Coca-Cola on ice to go, went out to my car, and drove to work. I was about halfway to the aluminum chair plant when Dinosaur, driving a Ford Mustang, pulled up behind me. The other three guys were in the car with him. They followed me to work. I parked close to the door and got out with my chips and Coca-Cola. I slurped at the Coca-Cola through a straw as I walked. I was saving the chips for dinner break. It was a light dinner, but I'd been trying to drop a few pounds. I was always prone to picking up weight, and I had to watch it.

I turned at the door into the plant and looked at them.

Dinosaur shot me the finger.

I shot him the finger back.

We had really showed each other. Funny how that can make people so mad. It's their finger in the air, and that's it. It has about as much actual effect as a leaf falling from a cherry tree in Japan.

They drove way, screeching tires as they left, and I went to work.

Next few days in school I'd see them in the hall, and I never once avoided them or tried to get out of the way.

They were not always together, though sometimes they were, and Dinosaur bumped me a couple of times as he went by. I kept my cool. Once David said to me as he passed, "We'll get you, nigger-lover."

This went on for a while, and now and then they'd follow me to work, but they never did anything. I had a ball bat in my car, and they knew that, because I let them see it by holding it up once while driving, knowing they could see it from their Mustang, as they were so close on my ass. What I feared is they'd hold up a gun or guns in response, but that didn't happen. Everyone wasn't shooting everybody back then.

This went on through the semester, and then the spring came, and one day I went downtown to buy some blue jeans and a union shirt. The old white union shirts had become popular. Everyone was dying them, or tie-dying them, and I guess I didn't want to be left out. What we had there in Marvel Creek was a kind of general store named Jack Woolens, and that's where I went to buy the shirt, couple pairs of jeans, and maybe what we called desert boots, which were tan, low-cut, comfortable shoes. I thought I had enough to afford it all. I was thinking on that, figuring I could skip one pair of pants if I had to, and I'd have enough for sure that way to get the shirt, shoes, and one pair of Lee Riders.

My hair had grown longer, and I had to comb it behind my ears at school and push it up off my forehead into a pompadour so I didn't get sent home. A bunch of us were wearing our hair longer, and there was even talk of a sit-in to protest how we were hassled by the principal, but I was the only one that showed up for the event. I ended up wandering around in the hall for a few minutes and went back to the lunchroom and had some Jell-O before going to math class. I had it washed and combed out this day, and it was bouncing loosely as I walked. I thought I was as cool as a razor edge in winter time.

I parked my junker and was walking along the sidewalk, almost to Jack Woolens. I could see the wooden barrels setting out front—one had walking canes in it and brooms, the other had axe and hoe handles.

As I came along the sidewalk, I saw Leonard coming toward me. He saw me and smiled. We hadn't seen each other in a while, but when I saw him I knew I had missed him. He was like a stray dog that wandered in and out of my life, and I felt like when we were together that something missing was fulfilled. It was an odd combo, him being a homo and me being straight, him being black and me being white, and him being more redneck than I was. He didn't like my long hair and had told me, and I didn't like that he thought we needed a conservative president. He was a stray dog I liked, and I decided right then and there I wanted to keep him, even if he might bite. He probably thought I was the stray dog. I doubt he worried about my bite, however. He came down the sidewalk with one hand in his pants pocket, the other swinging by his side.

That's when David and Dinosaur, and the other two thugs, got out of the Mustang parked across the street, having spotted me and caught me without my ball bat. They came across the street, almost skipping.

They got to me before Leonard.

They came up on the curb and managed their way around me in a half circle. The door to Jack Woolens was at my back. It was open. It was a cool day and air-conditioning wasn't as common then, so it was left that way to let in the breeze as well as too many flies.

"Gotcha now," David said.

"Gotcha what?" Leonard said, as he came up the sidewalk, both hands swinging by his sides now.

"You're the other one we want to see," said Dinosaur. "You and the girl, here."

"Wow," I said. "That bites. You see, Leonard, they're calling me a girl because my hair is long."

"It is too long," Leonard said.

"They are really pushing the wit, calling me a girl, noticing I have long hair. These guys, they ought to be on Johnny Carson."

"Fuck you," Dinosaur said.

"You're looking for us, well, you done found us," Leonard said.

"That's right," I said. "You have."

"We don't like what we see," David said.

"That's because you are a blind motherfucker and don't know a couple pretty fellas when you see them," Leonard said. "I could be on a fucking magazine, I'm so pretty. Shit. You could hang my goddamn dick in the museum of fucking modern art. Damn, Big Pile, you know you want to kiss my black ass, right where the tunnel goes down into the sweet dark depths."

"You gag me," David said.

"Fuck you," Dinosaur said.

"The big man is consistent with those two words," I said.

I didn't know what it was about Leonard, but he brought out the double smartass in me. I figured if I was going to die, I might as well go out with a few good remarks. And with Leonard there, well, I felt I had a chance. That we had a chance.

Leonard looked at me. "Yeah. He repeats himself because it's wishful thinking that slips out. Some of that Freudian stuff. Big white boy wants a piece of my fine, shiny, black ass I tell you, but his little ole dick dropped down there would be like tossing a noodle into a volcano."

"Now I'm starting to get gagged," I said.

"Ah, you'll get over it, Hap," Leonard said.

David said to Leonard, "You're a goddamn dick-sucking nigger and he's a nigger-lover."

"Nah," Leonard said. "I mean, yeah. I'm a dick-sucker, but me and Hap, we ain't fucking, just hanging. Oh, I should also add, I don't like being called a nigger, you cracker motherfucker."

"You got some sand," David said.

"I'm a whole goddamn beach," Leonard said.

"What we're thinking," David said, "is we're going to knock you two around until your shit mixes, until you get it through your head how things are supposed to be."

"That a fact?" I said.

"Oh yeah," Dinosaur said, "we're gonna do that."

Leonard grinned, said, "I guess you boys ought to get started. It's already midday."

"But the sun stays up for quite a while," I said.

"Yeah, there's that," Leonard said. "We got plenty of time to whip their asses."

"Smartass nigger," David said, and glanced at Dinosaur, who moved forward.

That's when an older black man stepped out of Jack Woolens and reached in one of the barrels and pulled out an axe handle.

"I hear you peckerwoods calling my nephew a nigger?" the man said.

David bowed up a little. "We ain't got a thing against hitting an old nigger, or a lady nigger, or kicking around a dead nigger, which is what you're gonna be, you ancient watermelon fart."

That's when the old man swung the axe handle and clipped David across the jaw and made him stagger. I almost felt sorry for David. Even more so when the handle whistled again and caught him behind the neck and laid him out flat on his face on the cement.

The other three thugs froze, then seemed to come unstuck and started toward the three of us. Me and Leonard took fighting stances. That's when Jack Woolens came out behind us, a slightly paunchy old man with thinning dark hair.

"Stop it, goddamnit," Jack said.

53

They stopped, but when Dinosaur saw who it was, he said, "You old Jew bastard."

"Old Jew bastard fought Nazis, so he isn't afraid of your kind. You aren't a pimple on a Nazi's ass, but you're made of the same kind of pus."

This stopped them. I don't know why, but they hesitated.

The old Jew bastard pulled an axe handle from the barrel and stepped up beside the black man. "Way I see it," he said, "is we have axe handles, and for now, you have teeth. You see it that way, Chester?"

Chester said, "Yeah. They got some teeth right now."

Dinosaur looked a little nervous. "We ain't even eighteen, and that nigger hit David with an axe handle."

"Hard as he could," Leonard said.

"That's against the law," Dinosaur said. "We're underage. Minors."

"Sometimes, you have extenuating circumstances," Jack Woolens said. "I once strangled a Nazi when I was in the OSS. Look it up, you never heard of it. It wasn't a social group. I strangled him and went back to the farmhouse where I was hiding in Austria, and slept tight. I knocked me off a piece the next day. Young German girl who thought I was German. I can speak it. I had the chance, I'd have strangled another fucking Nazi."

"No shit?" Chester said. "You speak German?"

It was like they forgot the thugs were there.

"Yeah, I was born in Germany."

"No shit?"

"Yeah. I did get a little scratch when I was strangling that Nazi by the way. I don't want to sound like I come out clean. That would be lying."

Jack Woolens put the axe handle back in the barrel, and showed Chester a cut across his elbow by nodding at it. It was a long white line.

"Knife," Jack said. "I had to wear a bandage for a few days."

"That ain't shit," Chester said. "Cracker tried to castrate me once. I got a scar on my thigh I can show you makes that look like hen scratch. I had twenty-five stitches and had to stand when I fucked for a while and reach under and hold my balls up so it didn't slap my stitches. Want to see?"

"You win," Jack said. "Keep your pants on."

"I was moving when the cracker did that, cut me, I mean," Chester said. "Cracker didn't turn out so well. They found his lily-white ass in the river, and there wasn't no way of knowing how he got there. Some kind of accident like being beat to death and thrown in the river is my guess. You know, said the wrong thing to someone, tried to cut their balls off, something like that. I ain't saying I know that to be a fact, him being dead in the Sabine River, but I'm going to start a real hard rumor about it right now."

Jack turned back to the barrel and retrieved the axe handle, casual as if he were picking out a toothpick.

The thugs continued to stand there. As if just remembering the thugs were there, Chester thumped Dinosaur's chest with the axe handle. "Pick up this sack of dog shit, and carry him off. Do it now, 'cause you don't, it'll be hard to do with broke legs. You boys carry him now, you won't have to scoot and pull him away with your teeth, ones you got left. Gumming him might be difficult. One way or another, though, it ain't gonna turn out spiffy for you fellows."

Dinosaur looked at me, then Leonard, then the older men. He looked at his friends. Nobody bowed up. No smart remarks were made. Dinosaur seemed small right then. They picked up David like he was a dropped puppet, tried to get him to stand, but they might as well have been trying to teach a fish how to ride a tricycle. They had to drag him across the street and into their car.

When they got David inside, the others got in, and Dinosaur went around to the driver's side. He shot us the finger. He said, "This ain't over."

"Better be," Jack Woolens said.

Dinosaur drove his friends out of there.

"We could have handled it," Leonard said.

"Maybe," I said.

"Shit," Leonard said. "We could."

"Now they're tough guys," Jack said to Chester. "It's all over, and now they're tough."

"We were tough enough," Leonard said, "and we could have got tougher."

"Leonard," Chester said, pulling car keys out of his pocket. "Bring the car around, and don't squeal the god-damn tires."

"Like he can't walk a few feet," Jack said. "Like he's

56

got a lot to carry. A pair of shoes on lay-a-way he bought. He can walk."

I looked at Leonard and he grinned at me. I loved that grin.

Chester said. "I got the lumbago."

"Lumbago," Jack said. "Now the lumbago he gets."

Chester grunted, said to Leonard, "Get the car, kid."

Leonard looked at me, smiled, and went away to get it.

4.
DOWN BY THE RIVERSIDE

We left the Dairy Queen, but neither of us wanted to go home. My gal Brett and my daughter Chance, along with our dog, Buffy, had gone out of town for the weekend, a drive to Houston to see Vince White and Kasey Lansdale perform in a small venue there. Dogs were allowed if they were well behaved and wore a muzzle, so that was part of the draw. They would be home tonight, but not right away, so we didn't feel any urge to rush home.

Me and Leonard wanted to go as well. Kasey Lansdale is one of Leonard's special favorites. We had this deal we were doing at the agency, but then after my girls left for the gig it fell through, the job we were supposed to have following this guy, and so we ended up with nothing special to occupy us. Sometimes, though, that's the best thing in the world there is to do. Nothing.

We needed and liked time to ourselves now and again. It was like old times when it was only the two of us.

As we drove about talking, we left LaBorde, and I guess it was instinct that drove me to my old home town of Marvel Creek. A little burg of four thousand or so, the place where I grew up and where I had a few adventures before graduating high school and leaving. Actually, I came back once and had what I guess you could call an adventure. The end of it was back at Leonard's place outside of LaBorde, and some people died. Badly. Leonard and I almost got a ticket too.

I didn't like thinking about that, because then I thought about my ex-wife, Trudy, and that depressed me. I loved Brett dearly, more than any other woman in my life, but Trudy, she was the first, and though I realized in time (too slow a time, actually) she was a manipulative shit, she had a place in my heart, deeply buried there like some kind of inoperable tumor.

Yet, here I was in Marvel Creek, thinking back on things, back on East Texas, back on the rough kind of life that was below the surface, the stuff that the people with money didn't know about, or didn't want to talk about. There were people back in the sixties, during the civil rights era, who said, "Oh, we all just got along fine. Black and white. They stayed over there, and we stayed right here. But I had nigger friends. We waved at each other in town."

We crossed the long Sabine bridge that led into Marvel Creek. The moon was on the water.

I said, "I've had a few experiences on that river. You and me have had a few experiences."

"Oh, yeah," Leonard said.

"I quit a friend one day on the Sabine," I said.

"What's that mean, quit a friend?"

We were coming back from fishing in the river with cane poles, and we were carrying the poles back to our car. We had parked it up away from the river, because down close it was muddy, and we didn't want to bog. We were sixteen, me and my friend Davis, though on that very day I decided I didn't want to be his friend anymore.

When we finished putting minnows on our hooks and stopped trying to catch fish, it was the fisherman's custom to pour the surviving minnows out of the bucket and into the river. I was about to do that when Davis came over and took hold of the handle of the foam bucket, pulled it from me, and poured the minnows on the ground, and then with a kind of savage delight, he stomped the little fish into the mud. I suppose it sounds odd to be sad about fish I would have put on my hook had the day not ran out and the fish been biting, but it always seemed to me that if you weren't going to use something for bait to catch something to eat, then you let it go. That was the way Dad did it and everyone I knew that fished.

But Davis didn't see it that way. He was laughing

while he did it, his eyes wide and wet-looking. He even tossed the foam bucket up and kicked it into the river like a football.

"Why the hell did you do that?" I said.

"I don't know," he said. "Fuck those minnows."

In that instant when he looked at me and his eyes latched on mine, I think he knew what I knew right then. We were done. Our friendship was over. I suppose it wasn't that one thing that ended it, but it was the one thing that capped it. I picked up my pole and started walking back to the car, and he carried his and we walked in silence up the trail through the woods and on out to where there were fewer trees.

There was a black car parked where the land rose up, and when we got there we saw two men, and then we could see there was another car, a white one, a little farther up on the hill. The men were standing out by the black car and there was a woman in the backseat and she sat there quietly with the windows open and the daylight fading. She was crying.

The men were hard looking, a little fat, and both had their hair heavily greased with hair oil; they looked a lot alike.

I said to the men, "Is she alright?"

"She's fine," one of them said. "Go on and mind your own business."

"I didn't mean nothing, mister," I said.

"Sure you didn't. It's okay. Just go on now."

I stopped and kept looking, feeling uncomfortable

about the whole thing, but Davis said, "Come on, man. Let's go."

The woman turned and looked at us. She was dark haired and pretty and her face was streaked with eye make-up and her lips trembled.

"Go on now," said the man again.

We went on up the hill and to my car which was farther up than the white car. It was parked off the path and under some trees near the long bridge that went over the Sabine. The men probably hadn't seen it. We had come there with our fishing poles stuck out the right back window and down by the sides of the passenger seat in the front, but when we got ready to go, we decided to toss the poles. They had lines and sinkers and hooks on them, and we had forgotten a small, plastic box of fishing gear down by the river. I thought about going back to get it, but knew I would have to pass by the car again, and the idea of it bothered me, so we just left everything.

"You think that woman's alright?" I said.

"They're out here fucking, Hap. Don't you know a damn thing?"

"Two of them?"

"Could have been ten of them, and they would still be out here fucking. She probably wanted it and then she got it and she didn't want it anymore. She might be making some money."

"I don't know," I said.

"You go on back down there you want, but I'm staying up here. It's just some woman that changed her mind too late. If it was me and I brought her all the way out here and she was okay with it and then changed her mind, she'd be in trouble, because if she got me this far with the idea of doing it, and she didn't, well, she's going to do it."

I thought about that, and there was no reason for me to think of it any other way than how Davis said about the men, though I didn't like what he said he'd do if it had been him and the woman didn't want to do what he wanted. We got in the car and I drove us out of there.

I dropped Davis off at his house, and though I saw him in school from time to time, we only spoke in a passing manner, and never went anywhere together again, and when I was in a place where he was I was uncomfortable.

I didn't think any more about the car and the men and the woman until some ten years later when I was home visiting my parents, and in the little town paper was an article about how an old black car had been fished out of the Sabine River the day before, and there was what was left of a body, bone fragments and a skull, in the car and no one knew who it was.

I didn't know her name. But I knew who it was.

5.
SHORT NIGHT

In Marvel Creek, in search of another ice cream cone, I drove us out to the Dairy Queen where I used to go, where all us kids used to go, not to eat, but just to have something to do. It was gone. There was a ragged used car lot there now.

"It's gone," I said.

"Just think," Leonard said, "those used cars are leaking oil right where you used to eat burgers."

"I guess it wasn't any kind of shrine," I said. "But it hurts that it's gone. Come back, I sort of think it ought to be there, but it isn't."

"You don't need another ice cream anyway."

I turned alongside where the Dairy Queen use to be and drove a back road. Once upon a time it had been nothing more than a blacktop and there weren't all the houses then. There were woods and there was swamp, and then you came to the river. The river was still there, but there were houses all along the shore. Most of the trees were gone. Where once their roots went deep, concrete covered the earth in shallow slabs. It was hard to realize that the place had been so thick with trees at one time that it was always in shadow, and the mosquitoes were thick in the summer time. You could go down there and hide out, or die, and never be found, and someone standing right next to you might not see you if you didn't want to be seen. Now, you had no place to hide.

"There used to be a place out here, above where we are now, where there used to be a hill with trees on it, and a clearing at the very top of the hill. They called it Humper's Hill. Drive out here on Friday, Saturday night, there'd be a half-dozen cars parked, all of them rocking. Now the trees are gone, and so is the hill. They leveled it. The energy it must have taken to level it, to cut all those trees, and just to put up all these boxes that look just alike."

"I was never part of that culture," Leonard said. "We queers . . . gays, humped in greater privacy because we didn't want straight, religious crackers, god-fearing assholes, to cut our dicks off. Mainly, I figured I'd have ended up killing someone. So the few interludes I had with others of my needs were in motels, or homes, now and again some place we could park, but not a community fuck park."

"It wasn't always dates, your best girl. Sometimes it

was just plain old nasty, hormonal driven stuff. Guys would bring some girl, or woman, wanted to make a few bucks and they'd pull the train. Demeaning stuff all around."

"You are so sensitive."

"I guess I am. Even though the lady was doing it of her own free will, it was all so tawdry, someone you didn't know spreading their legs in the back of a car and a bunch of guys standing around in line, waiting their turn."

"You must have been out here to know about it," Leonard said.

"You could know without being here, but yeah, I was here once when that was happening. For some guys it was a weekly thing."

"So tell me about the time you were here."

"Alright, and there's more to this one than just being out here on Humper's Hill. Fact is you're kind of included in this story."

"Alright, it's your turn," Ed said, and lit a cigarette.

"I don't think so," I said.

"Everyone else has done her."

"I can see that."

The back passenger door of the car opened and Jack climbed out pulling up his pants, swinging his dong like the pendulum inside a grandfather clock. He took his time to tuck it into place behind his jeans and fasten his belt. He was pretty proud of his dick, and had the nick name Horse.

"I'm all done," Jack said.

"You was done before you got started," a female voice from inside the car said.

"I did alright," Jack said.

"Sure you did," she said.

Jack coughed and sidled off to the back of the car and leaned on the trunk and looked at the moon as if it were his job to study the arrangement of craters.

Ed put his arm around my shoulders and walked me to the car and the open door.

"You might as well knock some off," Ed said. He was kind of the co-coordinator of the event.

"It's alright, hon," Billie Sue said from inside the car. "I don't mind."

"I can see that," I said.

"Oh come on," she said. "I said I could fuck you all, and you're the last one left."

"Fuck Jack twice," I said.

"Ah come on," she said. "He barely managed it the first time."

"To hell with you, you old whore," Jack said.

"Flattery will get you nowhere," she said.

Jack walked away from the car to the edge of the woods and took his horse dick out again and took a piss.

I looked in the car.

Billie Sue was big and fat and her belly heaved. Her legs were spread and what I could see was less inviting than a leap into the bayou at night. You couldn't be sure what was down there. I looked away and felt ashamed of myself for being out there in the first place.

Billie Sue was married to a Baptist preacher, and she liked to take a break from gospel singing and collecting the Lottie Moon offering to come out in the woods and fuck the senior class. Lottie Moon was a missionary who bothered the Chinese by trying to convert them. She was a kind of Baptist hero, but for me she was a long dead busybody. Billie Sue had been doing her own form of missionary work amongst each year's seniors for some four to five years. It was well known around town that she liked to bump with the boys, but her husband was said to give one damn fine sermon. The Baptists didn't want to lose him. And the knowledge of what his wife did made everyone in the congregation feel good about themselves. A little adultery and hypocrisy was easier to accept in one's self if the preacher's wife was considerably more wicked than they were. I thought that was nice. The Church of Christ had fired their preacher because he got caught dancing at a honky-tonk.

"Come on, kid, hop on," Billie Sue said. "I've got my second wind."

"No disrespect to you," I said. "Know you're trying to break a record, but I just came out here to see the stars."

"The stars?" Billie Sue said, and laughed.

"Well, I didn't come for this," I said.

"Shit," Ed said. "You come for something, and it wasn't any stars. I think you ain't got the wood in your pencil to do it."

"Now that I've seen what I'm supposed to do, and who's gone before me, I'll admit there might be a severe lack of wood."

"You queer?" Billie Sue said, sat up and rested her back against the door on the far side.

"No."

"Free pussy and you ain't taking any?" Jack said. He had wandered back over. "That sounds queer to me."

"Jack's trying to get back on my good side," Billie Sue said.

Mike, a guy I knew a little, moved away from the other boys who were drinking beer near the back of the car, came over to me, said to Jack and Ed, "Leave him be. It wasn't any good anyway."

"Fuck you," Billie Sue said.

"I've had better when I didn't have any," Mike said.

"What's that supposed to mean?" Billie Sue said.

"It means it stunk."

"Well hell," she said, "by the time you was there, there had been eight others."

"That explains it then," Mike said. "Come on, Hap. Let's go."

"I didn't bring a car," I said.

"He came with me," Ed said. "I knew he was going to embarrass me like this, I wouldn't have brought him."

"It's alright," Billie Sue said. "I don't expect to be universally admired."

"You deserve respect," Ed said. "He can walk home, all I care."

"I got a car," Mike said.

I went with Mike and he drove us out of there in his '62 Impala.

We rode down off the hill, out of the night, into the glowing lights of the houses along the way, and then into the brighter lights of the Dairy Queen by the highway. Mike parked in the Dairy Queen lot and we went inside, ordered hamburgers and Cokes. Mike went to the bathroom while the burgers were cooking. I picked us a table at the rear of the place and sat down. There was no one else there but us and the cook and the fellow at the register. Mike came back, sat, and said, "I really needed to wash up. I touched her a little. Not on purpose, but trying to guide it in, you know?"

"Okay," I said.

"I'm not trying to make you feel bad about not doing it," he said.

"I don't feel bad."

"She's okay with it," Mike said. "She likes it fine. It's a hobby."

"I know."

"She did ten guys last year, and this year she was going for twelve. She did eleven."

"Guess I messed up her record."

"She really had her heart set on twelve."

"Life is full of little disappointments," I said.

The burgers and drinks were called. We went up and got them and brought them back to the table.

"That stuff they said, about you being queer out there," Mike said, and turned his head a little when he spoke again. "You know, you're like that, it's okay with me. I've known a few. My uncle Bill was that way. One time I caught him sucking a school teacher's dick in our living room. He thought I was out, but I was in the bedroom reading. My uncle was a teacher too. He taught art. The guy's dick he was sucking, I don't remember what he taught. Speech or something."

"No. I'm not like that," I said.

"You know that colored fella you hang with?"

"Leonard?"

"He's queer."

"I know."

"It bother you?" Mike asked. "Not him being colored, but the queer part."

"Some at first. I guess I didn't know what to make of it. He seems like everyone else to me, except for the dick-sucking part. He doesn't hide it any. I figure he'll get killed on account of it. Hell, I might get killed on account of it, I keep hanging around with him. I like him though. He's one tough sucker. He can be funny."

"I don't think of him as funny."

"He can be."

"I think it would take one tough customer to kill that nigger," Mike said.

"I don't think he likes being called a nigger. I'd stick with colored."

"That's something, ain't it. Don't call him nigger, but queer is alright."

"I think he does say he's queer. Says it plain and simple. I think he wouldn't want someone else to call him that, though. I know I wouldn't advise it."

"About the queer stuff, don't misunderstand me. I don't mind he is. Shit, right circumstances, I'd try it."

"What?"

"Sucking a dick."

"Oh."

"You?" he asked, and buried his face in his hamburger.

"Not on your life," I said. "I'm okay Leonard wants to do it. He's my friend. But I don't want no snapshots of it, diagrams and such. I like pussy just fine. Just didn't like that one tonight. I'm ashamed I went out there. I don't know what the hell I was thinking. I sure wouldn't want my girlfriend to know I went out there."

"You have a girlfriend?"

"Not right now. But if I had one, I wouldn't want her to know."

"Course not," Mike said, and nodded his head. "Understand, I was just posing a possible situation. A what if. I wasn't suggesting you and me might do such a thing. Suck each other's dick, I mean."

I got it then. I said, "But you fucked her."

He cleared his throat a little and took a sip of Coke.

"Yeah," he said. "Sure. It was fine. She was fat and a

little sticky, but it was fine. I didn't mean what you think I meant. That wasn't what I was talking about. Not really. I was just talking."

"Sure," I said.

"Don't say anything to anybody," he said. "They might get the wrong idea."

"No problem."

"Hey, I'll drop you off."

"Thanks," I said.

We finished our burgers without talking and went out to his car.

He drove us away. He knew where I lived.

"How about the team this year?" he said. "I think we're going to stomp shit out of Mineola."

"It could happen," I said, as if I knew the first thing about football. I'd been to one game and that was so I could watch a girl I liked lead the cheers. She left with a football player and I left with some popcorn.

When Mike pulled up in my yard he cut the headlights so they didn't shine in the house windows and stir my parents. I opened my door, and that turned on the overhead light. I said, "Thanks for the ride. See you later."

"Hey, just to be clear," he said, "I was just kidding earlier, but it might have sounded like, you know—"

"No," I said. "It's good. I get it."

He looked at me there in the glow of the overhead light. He knew I got it alright.

I wanted to say something else to him, but I couldn't

come up with anything. I closed the door and he drove away. It was for a weekend, a short night.

I saw him at school after that. He always smiled and said hi, but he never sat with me at lunch, and he didn't spend any time with me when we crossed paths. After a while I didn't see him around anymore and I heard later from Leonard that he moved off to some place up north with his family.

6.
THE BOY WHO BECAME INVISIBLE

By the time I finished telling Leonard all about it, I had turned us around and was driving back through town. We passed the old high school. It had been built during the Great Depression by the WPA. It was still solid, with a tall tower. I couldn't remember what was in the tower anymore. Maybe I never knew. It sure wasn't a classroom. Offices maybe.

They had built a new school farther out on the edge of town, but I wasn't sure why. The way this one had been built, it was sturdy and could have gone on forever. Maybe the plumbing was bad. It was empty now. I stopped in front of it and we rolled the windows down. A wind was blowing and it blew against the building and made a whistling sound up high around the tower and rattled the leaves on a large hickory tree that still grew out front.

I had my picture taken there when I was in high school, something or another for the yearbook.

I started us up again, and we edged around the high school, back to where there used to be a tennis court. There was now a house, and a not a very good one. Poor people house. I had lived in many of them, leaky roofs, slow-flush toilets, interruptions in electrical service due to payment being slow.

"Right back there, under that walk, at the door you see coming out of the old school, something terrible happened. Something I sometimes feel I had a part in."

I pulled over to the curb where we could see the place I was talking about, between the house and an empty space where the phys-ed building once stood. Now it was an empty lot thick with weeds.

"You're all memory lane tonight, aren't you?" Leonard said.

"Sorry."

"Hard to believe there are things you haven't told me about, long as we've known each other."

"Some I haven't mentioned to anyone in years. Some I guess I kind of forgot. Tonight, I remember all kinds of stuff, or maybe I'm letting myself remember."

"I doubt you ever really forgot it," Leonard said. "I know I got a few things tucked away."

"You're right. It's always there."

"I know you want to tell me what happened," Leonard said. "So why don't you?"

The place where I grew up was a little town called Marvel Creek. Not much happened there that is well remembered by anyone outside of the town. But things went on, and what I'm aware of now is how much things really don't change. We just know more than we used to because there are more of us, and we have easier ways to communicate excitement and misery than in the old days.

Marvel Creek was nestled along the edge of the Sabine River, which is not a wide river, and as rivers go, not that deep, except in rare spots, but it is a long river, and it winds all through East Texas. Back then there were more trees than now, and where wild animals ran, concrete and houses shine bright in the sunlight.

Our little school wasn't much, and I hated going. I liked staying home and reading books I wanted to read, and running the then-considerable woods and fishing the creeks for crawdads. Summers and afternoons and weekends I did that with my friend Jesse. I knew Jesse's parents lived differently than we did, and though we didn't have money, and would probably have been called poor by the standards of the early sixties, Jesse's family still lived out on a farm where they used an outhouse and plowed with mules, raised most of the food they ate, drew water from a well, but, curiously, had electricity and a big tall TV antenna that sprouted beside their house and could be adjusted for better reception by reaching through the living room window and turning it with a twist of the hands. Jesse's dad was quick to use the razor strop on Jesse's butt and back for things my parents would have thought unimportant, or at worst an offense that required words, not blows.

Jesse and I liked to play Tarzan, and we took turns at it until we finally both decided to be Tarzan, and ended up being Tarzan twins. It was a great mythology we created and we ran the woods and climbed trees, and on Saturday we watched *Jungle Theater* at my house, which showed, if we were lucky, Tarzan or Jungle Jim movies, and if not so lucky, Bomba movies.

About fifth grade there was a shift in dynamics. Jesse's poverty began to be an issue for some of the kids at school. He brought his lunch in a sack, since he couldn't afford the cafeteria, and all his clothes came from the Salvation Army. He arrived at history class one morning wearing socks with big S's on them, which stood for nothing related to him, and they immediately became the target of James Willeford and Ronnie Kenn. They made a remark about how the S stood for Sardines, which would account for how Jesse smelled, and sadly, I remember thinking at that age that was a pretty funny crack until I looked at Jesse's slack, white face and saw him tremble beneath that patched Salvation Army shirt.

Our teacher came in then, Mr. Waters, and he caught part of the conversation. He said, "Those are nice socks you got there, Jesse. Not many people can have monogrammed socks. It's a sign of sophistication, something a few around here lack."

It was a nice try, but I think it only made Jesse feel all the more miserable, and he put his head down on his desk and didn't lift it the entire class, and Mr. Waters didn't say a word to him. When class was over, Jesse was up and out, and as I was leaving, Mr. Waters caught me by the arm. "I saw you laughing when I came in. You been that boy's friend since the two of you were knee-high to a legless grasshopper."

"I didn't mean to," I said. "I didn't think."

"Yeah, well, you ought to."

That hit me pretty hard, but I'm ashamed to say not hard enough.

I don't know when it happened, but it got so when Jesse came over I found things to do. Homework, or some chore around the house, which was silly, because unlike Jesse, I didn't really have any chores. In time he quit stopping by, and I would see him in the halls at school, and we'd nod at each other, but seldom speak.

The relentless picking and nagging from James and Ronnie continued, and as they became interested in girls, it increased. And Marilyn Townsend didn't help either. She was a lovely young thing and as cruel as they were.

One day, Jesse surprised us by coming to the cafeteria with his sack lunch. He usually ate outside on one of the stoops, but he came in this day and sat at a table by himself, and when Marilyn went by he watched her, and when she came back with her tray, he stood up and smiled, politely asked if she would like to sit with him.

She laughed. I remember that laugh to this day. It was as cold as a knife blade in the back and easily as sharp. I saw Jesse's face drain until it was white, and she went on by laughing, not even saying a word, just laughing, and pretty soon everyone in the place was laughing, and Marilyn came by me, and she looked at me, and heaven help me, I saw those eyes of hers and those lips, and whatever made all the other boys jump did the same to me . . . and I laughed.

Jesse gathered up his sack and went out.

It was at this point that James and Ronnie came up with a new approach. They decided to treat Jesse as if he were a ghost, as if he were invisible. We were expected to do the same. So as not to be mean to Jesse, but being careful not to burn my bridges with the in-crowd, I avoided him altogether. But there were times, here and there, when I would see him walking down the hall, and on the rare occasions when he spoke, students pretended not to hear him, or James would respond with some remark like, "Do you hear a duck quacking?"

When Jesse spoke to me, if no one was looking, I would nod.

This went on into the ninth grade, and it became such a habit, it was as if Jesse didn't exist, as if he really were invisible. I almost forgot about him, though I did note in math class one day there were stripes of blood across his back, seeping through his old worn shirt. His father and the razor strop. Jesse had nowhere to turn.

One afternoon I was in the cafeteria, just about to get in line, when Jesse came in carrying his sack. It was the first time he'd been there since the incident with Marilyn some years before. I saw him come in, his head slightly down, walking as if on a mission. As he came near me, for the first time in a long time, for no reason I can explain, I said, "Hi, Jesse."

He looked up at me surprised, and nodded, the way I did to him in the hall, and kept walking.

There was a table in the center of the cafeteria, and that was the table James and Ronnie and Marilyn had claimed, and as Jesse came closer, for the first time in a long time, they really saw him. Maybe it was because they were surprised to see him and his paper sack in a place he hadn't been in ages. Or maybe they sensed something. Jesse pulled a small revolver from his sack and before anyone knew what was happening, he fired three times, knocking all three of them to the floor. The place went nuts, people running in all directions. Me, I froze.

Then, like a soldier, he wheeled and marched back my way. As he passed me, he turned his head, smiled, said, "Hey, Hap," then he was out the door. I wasn't thinking clearly, because I turned and went out in the hall behind him, and the history teacher, Mr. Waters, saw him with the gun, said something, and the gun snapped again, and Waters went down. Jesse walked all the way to the double front door, which was flung wide open at that time of day, stepped out into the light, and lifted the revolver. I heard it pop and saw his head jump and he went down. My knees went out from under me and I sat down right there in the hall, unable to move.

When they went out to tell his parents what had happened to him, that Marilyn was disfigured, Ronnie wounded, and James and Mr. Waters were dead, they discovered them in bed where Jesse had shot them in their sleep.

The razor strop lay across them like a dead snake.

7.
BLOOD AND LEMONADE

While we drove through Marvel Creek, I thought of my family living here, scraping out a living, my father working long hours, and my mother working part-time, and sometimes full-time, but when I was growing up she was at home with me, turning what might have been a dreary existence into something special. On rainy weekend days she made me glue with flour and water so I could paste my projects, she walked me in the woods and showed me what plants were edible. When there was very little to eat in the house, she could turn having a bowl of corn mush, a pot of pinto beans, a fried squirrel, or even a mayonnaise sandwich into what seemed like a culinary event.

And she was smart, a woman ahead of time, brought up in a sexist environment, a time when if women were disagreeable or hardworking they were bitches, or they were having their period, or it was all about hormones; they were being emotional, hysterical.

She was special.

I was nine years old when this happened, and I had gone to see some kind of monster movie followed by a couple of cowboy shows.

We got there early, me and my mother, and there was already a line of snot-nosed kids yakking it up and chewing gum, ready to give the lady at the ticket window their quarter for Saturday admission. The teenagers were having to drag out a whole thirty-five cents, 'cause you turned thirteen, the cost jumped a dime.

You got there on Saturday for what was called the Kid's Show, you got to see cartoons and a few old serials, not to mention a kid's show, usually some kind of monster movie or sword and sandal thing, and when that was over, you wanted to stay, and I always did, you could watch the double feature, and then keep your seat and watch both again. One would be the main feature, and the other a shorter running B-movie.

My mother had dropped me off at the library that morning, and I wandered the stacks and read until she picked me up at eleven-thirty, and I carried my four books I was allowed to check out from the library out to the car and we pretty much drove across the street and parked in front of the drugstore next to the theater. Back then, the drugstore served hamburger and soda drinks, and you could buy a hamburger for fifteen cents, a bag of chips for a nickel, a soft drink for the same—we called all soft drinks Cokes or Coca-Cola then. We'd say, "What kind of Coke do you want?" and you might choose an orange pop or a chocolate drink. It's how we talked.

My mother would buy me a hamburger, chips, and soda pop, and then when that was done, she'd walk me next door to the movies. I was getting old enough I preferred to do it myself, but she always insisted, as if by taking me she could slow down my growing up. Or maybe she just wanted to make sure I got safely inside, though where we lived there wasn't exactly a crime wave going on.

Next to the line where we were standing, there was another line at the same ticket booth, but at another ticket slot. This was for the black people, who at that time were referred to as colored, when being polite. Now and again, after helping several white kids, or sometimes helping them until the line of whites was down to nearly nothing, the lady in the ticket booth would turn to the other slot and take money and give tickets to the black people.

When they got their ticket they went up a shaky wooden staircase that led to the balcony, what I had been heard called the nigger's nest. I had seen this before, but for some reason, that day, it registered that they were always in the balcony, but never down in the floor seats.

I of course knew there was a separation of races and that black people were not looked upon with fondness by a lot of white people, but on that day, I suddenly wondered why it was such a big deal.

I remember clearly turning to my mother and saying, "Why are those people going up there?"

It was a totally innocent remark, and when I made it, I saw my mother pause, as if she had realized one of her shoes had been nailed to the floor. A lump was in her throat. She said, "I can't explain it to you, son. But it's not right, and it won't always be that way."

That's all the discussion we had on the matter, because now I had my ticket. I went into the show, as we called it, and had probably forgotten all about it by the time I got to the concession counter. A hamburger, chips, and drink hadn't stopped me from wanting popcorn and another soda pop, and maybe some candy. Mom had given me enough money for that, and though I was supposed to wait until during the previews between the kid show and the first movie, the B feature, I bought my stuff right away. Unlike some of the other kids, I really loved movies and I loved previews and going to the show was akin to visiting a religious shrine. I even enjoyed watching the advertisements that encouraged a trip to the concession stand.

The theater was pleasantly air-conditioned and had a sticky aisle carpet that sucked at your shoes, and many of the seats were missing the arm rest, and therefore sometimes your arms rested on bolts. But that air-conditioning made it a great place to be during the summer even if the movie was some kind of love story.

The screen was stained in spots and there was a stage in front of it where sometimes magicians performed kid shows, and occasionally there were jugglers and dog acts.

I made it all the way through the kid show monster movie, the double feature, and was there when it started over, when my mother came down the aisle and tapped me on the shoulder.

I wanted to see the shows again, because back then you didn't have to leave during showings, but she insisted I had to go, and so we went out to the curb where our car was parked. It was dark by then, but the theater lights were bright behind us, and there were lights along the walk, in front of the drugstore and other businesses, so it was easy to see a little black boy, crying in the drugstore doorway. I guess he was about my age.

Mom went over to him, said, "Are you okay, little boy?"

He looked up at her and sucked snot up in his nose, said, "I'm alright."

"You don't sound alright," Mom said.

"I got beat up."

"Who would do a thing like that?"

He shook his head. She bent down and looked at him. "You're bleeding."

Mama opened her purse and took out a Kleenex and dabbed at the blood on his face. "Who would do such a thing?"

"White boy done it," he said.

"A white boy beat you up?"

He nodded.

"Why would he do that?"

The boy looked at her in a puzzled way, as if she had just parachuted in from Venus.

"'Cause I'm a nigger."

"Don't call yourself that."

"He did."

"Yes. But that isn't right."

"He still called me one."

"Can we take you home?" Mom said.

"No. My mama lives out of town. Supposed to stay with my cousin, but he went off with a girl."

"How old is your cousin?"

"Eighteen."

"And he left you by yourself."

"He don't keep up with time so good."

"I can't believe he left you."

"I can, that's how he do."

"So there's no place we can take you?"

"Cousin's house is all locked up. I'd have to break a window."

"Aren't his parents home?"

He shook his head. "They don't live there no more, just him."

"Alright, alright," Mama said. "Well, look, we can't just leave you here in a doorway. Tell you what. Come home with us, and we'll call your mama and have her come get you."

"She ain't got no phone. Got a sister has one."

"Then we'll call her."

"She lives in another town, Overton."

"And your mother lives where?"

"Tyler, but she's gone to Dallas. That's why I was to stay with my cousin."

"Come on, then," Mama said. "You come with us and we'll call someone, figure something out."

Mama got his name out of him, Nathan, and with reluctance he climbed into the backseat of the car and sat there with his hands in his lap. He looked scared and confused, like a dog that had been left beside the road and wasn't sure of those who had found and taken him in.

I sat on the passenger side of the front seat, and tried not to stare over the backseat. When I did glance back, he always seemed to be looking at me, wild-eyed and nervous. In our old black Ford we clattered home. My dad was a mechanic, and a good one, but our car was always on the verge of falling apart. He had time to work on other cars, but when he had time off he wanted to lay down in front of the TV and relax. The car he drove to work was worse than the one Mama drove.

At home our guest came nervously through the front door between Mama and me as if expecting a surprise attack, and when Mama hit the light switch, he jumped a little.

"Why don't you go to the bathroom and wash up, and I'll fix you something to eat. Would you like that?"

Nathan didn't answer, just looked around. Our house wasn't much, and my mother was not a great housekeeper, but she painted, and she had several of her paintings on the walls. She was a pretty amazing hobby painter, but I didn't know it at the time. It's just what she did when she was on a kind of manic high. The high was followed by a lull, and then a drop into a depressed place where the walls around it were for a time too steep for her to climb.

"Those are pretty," Nathan said, pointing toward the paintings.

"Thank you," Mama said. "I painted those."

"You did?" Nathan said.

"I did."

"I ain't never known someone could do that. I wish I could."

"Practice," Mama said, and she went into the kitchen and left us standing there in the middle of the living room.

"Let me show you where the bathroom is," I said. "You can get that blood off your face."

I headed in that direction, and when I turned around in the hall, he wasn't there. I had to go back to the living room and say, "Nathan. Right here."

Nathan came unstuck from looking at the paintings,

went to the bathroom and closed the door. I stood out in the hall like a hall monitor at school. I didn't know what else to do. I could hear the water running in there. After a moment the door opened. Nathan said, "Are there any towels for me? I can wipe on my pants."

I found this curious, not knowing quite yet that anything a black person touched was supposedly contaminated, so I said, "Use the one hanging on the rack."

"Ain't that your towel?"

"It's a towel," I said.

"I got blood on me."

"It's alright," Mama called from the kitchen. "It'll wash."

"Okay," he said, went back inside and closed the door. After a few moments he came out again.

"You find the towel?"

He nodded, looked down the hallway. We could see my mama in the kitchen at the end, hustling around at the edge of the stove. She turned from it and came down the hall. She took Nathan's chin in her hand and gently turned his head from side to side.

"You might ought to have a band aid."

She got a box of them out of the bathroom cabinet and pulled one out, came out into the hall, and applied it to the small cut on Nathan's head.

"There now," she said. She went back to the bathroom, washed her hands, dried on a fresh towel, and went back to the kitchen.

"Your mama's nice," Nathan said.

"Yeah, she is. You like funny books?"

He looked at me and nodded.

I started for my bedroom. Nathan followed after me, still cautious.

We weren't well off, poor actually, but at this short time in my early life we had it pretty good. My dad was a mechanic. He worked for a butane company repairing their trucks, chasing them when they broke down in other parts of Texas, Oklahoma, and Louisiana. He might go to work in the morning and not be back until late at night, or even the next morning, having gone over to Many Louisiana, some place in Oklahoma or almost any place in Eastern Texas. Wherever a company truck might break down. Within a year of the time I'm talking about, Daddy would be worn out working for someone other than himself, and would end up opening his own shop. We never had much money after that, but he was happier, and to be honest, I didn't realize the difference much until I was grown and could look back on it. I didn't know we were poor. We always thought of ourselves as broke, but at that moment in time, we were doing as well as we ever did. There were so many others around us doing worse. Black families especially.

Nathan came into my bedroom, leaving the door open as if he might need to beat a hasty retreat. I opened my closet, and there were several large boxes there with comics stacked inside. I pulled one out, opened the box, and dug in. I grabbed a stack of funny books and we sat down on the floor. Nathan and I looked through them, and out of nowhere, he said, "I want to be the Flash. I could run off anywhere and no one would know I was gone, and then I'd be back, and they wouldn't even had known I'd run across the ocean, gone over to some place there, and come back."

"I like that he can run across the water," I said.

"Me too," Nathan said, "but I get to thinking about what if I was him, and I slowed down? I'd be wet all over and a shark might get me."

"Flash runs too fast to get bit," I said, "and he won't slow down, and you was him, you wouldn't either."

"Yeah, but I ain't him. He's white."

I realized I had never seen a black superhero, or for that matter, any black characters in comics. It had never occurred to me a black superhero was possible. I thought of most blacks as maids and short-order cooks, farmers and janitors. That's what they did in Marvel Creek. Those were their jobs.

"You boys come eat," Mama called from the kitchen. Through the open door we could see down the hall and into the kitchen. Mama was wearing an apron and hustling plates of food onto the table.

We went into the kitchen. I sat down immediately, but Nathan remained standing.

"Sit down," Mama said. "This isn't at the Dairy Queen or such. You don't have a special place where you have to be."

I got it a little more then. Nathan was not only unaccustomed to being with white folks, he was unaccustomed at being allowed to sit at their tables, instead of some designated spot for colored. I was starting to absorb the idea that being colored meant you always had to be on your toes.

Nathan sat down and Mama put a plate in front of him. There were some fried hamburger patties, slices of tomato, some broken up lettuce in bowls. We had plain light bread, as we used to call it, and she had busted open a loaf and laid the bread on a platter. There was a big pitcher of ice tea, a bottle of ketchup, and a jar of mustard.

Mama started making herself a sandwich with the bread, meat, and vegetables, and I followed suit. Nathan still hadn't moved.

"We got mustard and ketchup, you want it," Mama said.

"No, ma'am," Nathan said. "Dry is fine."

Then Nathan came unstuck and poured himself some ice tea, and made a sandwich. He would have gladly eaten in silence, I'm sure, but Mama didn't play that way.

"You finish eating, Nathan, maybe you got someone we can call?"

Nathan didn't respond to that.

I should add we had recently gotten a telephone, and for us that was a big deal. It was a party line, which meant we shared it with two others, had our own ring, and that meant, of course, that someone on the party line could listen into your conversations if they took a mind to. Now and again you could hear them breathing on their end. I remember Mama saying, "Mildred, get off the line. This is a private call."

Still, we had a phone, and it was a step up from where we had been. We also had a new TV, a larger set than the one before, and with two cars, ragged as they were, my parents probably felt they had stepped up in the world. It was a step that would become slippery in short time.

"We ain't got a phone, and my cousin don't neither, and I don't want to go where he stay anyway," Nathan said. "I'd be by myself if I could get in."

"I can understand that perfectly," Mama said. "I get by myself, I turn lonely. I like to at least be able to open a window, look out and see a bird, listen to it sing. Birds singing is a joy to me."

"Not many out at night," Nathan said.

Mama laughed. "Well, I don't mean now."

"Oh," Nathan said. "I get it. Some other time."

"Just something pleasant to see and think about," Mama said.

I glanced across the table at her, because when she said that, I saw something shift in her face. I had seen it before. She called it feeling blue. That meant a memory, or maybe just a feeling, had come up from some place deep and floated onto her face, wrinkling her brow, accentuating the crow's feet at the corners of her eyes.

"Sometimes I feel like I don't fit," she said.

"I know that," Nathan said. "I get that same way."

Mama looked at him, said, "I don't have anything on you, do I?"

"No ma'am," Nathan said. He sounded like an old man then, weighted down by memories and a touch of arthritis.

We finished eating, and Mama said, "Surely, you have someone I can call?"

"Mama ain't got no phone."

"Your cousin?"

"He don't got one neither."

"Surely there's someone? Didn't you say you had an aunt in Overton?"

Nathan considered for a long moment.

"She ain't never home," he said. "I got an aunt in Baton Rouge."

"Oh, that's a long ways," Mama said. "Still, I think I ought to call her."

Mama wrangled the aunt's number out of him and picked up the phone, which was on the kitchen counter under the light switch. She dialed the number and called the aunt.

No one answered. She put the phone down.

"You said your mama was in Dallas?"

"She ought to be back by now," Nathan said.

I glanced at the clock. It was nearly midnight.

"I'm thinking maybe I could drive you home, then," Mama said.

"I ain't sure how to get there," Nathan said.

"You got an address, something that could help me find her?"

He did have an address. Getting it out of him was like

trying to lift a car, but Mama finally managed and wrote it down.

"Tell you what," she said. "You boys go look at funny books. I'm going to get a Tyler map and see if I can figure out where this address is."

Back in my bedroom we went back to looking at funny books. Nathan had loosened up. We sat on the floor and talked about funny-book characters, and the movie we had seen that day. He liked the monster movie, and that led us to talking about other monster movies we had seen. It was great to have someone that cared about that stuff as much as me.

After a time, Mama came into the bedroom and said, "I think I got it figured out. We might have to pull over some and have me study the map, but I think we can go now."

"I could stay here tonight," Nathan said.

"I don't know, hon," Mama said.

"Oh, yeah," Nathan said. "I forgot."

"No," Mama said. "It's not that. You should be home. Your mama will be worried."

"She thinks I'm at my cousin's."

"But you're not, and she thinks you are," Mama said. "I don't think that's good."

There was an uncomfortable moment, and then Nathan said, "Yeah. I better go home."

"I'm going to pull the car out of the carport, you boys come out and we'll go."

I got up and prowled around in my closet and came up

with a stack of comic books, doubles of comics I already had. I gave them to Nathan.

"These for me?"

"Sure. I got some more."

"Thanks," he said. "You been real nice."

We went out to the car, not bothering to turn off the light or lock the door. We didn't lock doors much in those days. They used to say locks were for keeping honest people out, and lights make the bad folks think you're at home.

I sat in the backseat with Nathan. Mama looked back at me when I sat down back there, seemed as if she might say something, then didn't.

We drove out of Marvel Creek, over the Sabine River bridge. We drove past what was then called Hell's Half Mile, a series of honky-tonks. I remember driving by there with Dad at the wheel, and he said, "You see that tree out back of that beer joint? They hung a nigger there once, back in the forties. Reckon he wasn't but twelve years old. Raped some white girl. I used to have a postcard they made from a picture they took."

It was then that I was glad Dad was still at work, on the road somewhere. I couldn't imagine him being mean to Nathan. I had seen him do too many kind things for colored, and I would see more when he opened his own garage, working on their cars for free when they couldn't pay him, giving black kids money when we didn't have any. But still, it was then that I realized my mama and daddy lived in different worlds. When Dad had talked about that hanging, it sounded as if there was a bit of pride in his voice. Mama told me later, when she put me to bed that night, "His bark is worse than his bite. Your daddy's father used to tell your daddy when he went to bed at night, 'You do something wrong, a nigger's going to come get you and chop you up.' I'm just using the word they used, but I don't mean for you to say it. I want you to know how it was."

It was these sorts of things that gradually allowed me to understand how things were different between us and the colored. Mama was of her time, but not in the same way as everyone else. She could see a crack in the cloud cover, a ray of light, when all the others could see was an eternal black night.

That night we were driving Nathan home, we stopped along the way a few times, and Mama sat behind the wheel with the map and a flashlight on it, studying it. I don't know how long we drove, but it was longer than it would have taken had Nathan known how to get there, instead of just knowing the address.

Nathan and I both nodded off in the back seat, it was so comfortable, and when I awoke we had come to a dark part of town where there were no street lights and the houses seemed to tumble out of the dark beside the road.

"I don't see any street numbers," Mama said. "Maybe you ought to wake Nathan."

I touched his shoulder and he came awake quickly.

Mama, who was looking over the backseat, said, "Nathan, honey. I've got this far, but don't see street numbers or signs. Do you recognize this place?"

Nathan sat up and leaned over the seat and looked around. "Yes, ma'am, we about there."

He gave Mama some instructions then, and we proceeded down the street and turned on a narrow dirt street and pulled up at the edge of a dead, brown yard with a graying little house in it. There was a white Ford parked up on the grass near the front door.

Mama got out, and me and Nathan did too, Nathan with the funny books under his arm. He ran ahead of us and knocked on the door. Nothing happened, so he knocked again, louder.

Finally a heavy colored woman came to the door, opened it, stepped out onto the concrete steps. She looked out at us, then down to Nathan.

"What you doing here?" the woman said to Nathan. "You supposed to be at your cousin's house."

"He left me and some white kids beat me up," Nathan said.

"What? Come tomorrow, I'm going to drive over there to your cousin's house and tear his ass up. Who's this white lady?"

"I been at her house. Me and him read comics and she gave me dinner, drove me over here."

"That right?" said the woman.

"It was no trouble," my mama said.

"Ain't no one asking you to do it," Nathan's mother said.

This stunned Mama.

"I know. We were glad to do it."

"He don't need some white folks helping him out, showing him how kind you is. What's that under your arm, boy?"

"Funny books," Nathan said.

"Where you get them?"

"He gave them to me."

"Let me see those."

Nathan slowly handed the stack to her.

"Come here, white boy. Take these back."

"I gave them to him," I said.

"I don't care you did or didn't, come take them, or I'll tear them up."

I went over and took the stack from her and went back quickly to stand by Mama. We were still back a ways from the steps, and I was starting to feel really uncomfortable.

A colored man came to the door. He was big and stout and didn't have on a shirt.

"What's going on here?" he said.

"These white folks done brought Nathan home and was trying to give him some funny books."

"Johnny left me," Nathan said.

"He did," said the man. Then he looked out at us. "This is nice of you folks."

"No," said Nathan's mother. "It's just them showing us they got good ways. I tell you about y'all's good ways. Why don't you come on up in here tonight, spend the night with us, not drive back. Tomorrow, we can all go down to the sto' and shop for some groceries. We could then go to your house and have a tea party. You think that would be good? We can go to your church together this Sunday, and then you can come over here and we'll sit on the couch and watch TV. Maybe we'll go to the picture show, and you can sit up in the balcony with us."

Mama said, "We better go."

"Yeah, you better," the woman said.

"Now don't talk like that," the man said to the woman.

"I talk like I talk," she said.

"Thank y'all for bringing him home," he said to us.

"Yeah, y'all such do-gooders," said the woman. Then to Nathan, "Get your ass up in that house."

"Come on, son," Mama said, touched my shoulder, and headed to the car, walking fast.

"You come on back when you want that tea party," said the woman.

We got in the car. I sat in the front this time.

As we drove off, Mama started crying.

"Damn niggers," I said.

"Don't say that," she said, and pulled the car over. "Don't say that ever again. Never use that word about colored people. Colored or Negro. Don't you never say that."

"Daddy does," I said.

Mama was heaving a little, still crying. "Listen here. I've told you about that. Your daddy don't know any better, but you do. Hear me?"

"But she was mean."

"You walk a mile in her shoes, then you can judge. You got to see it from her side."

I didn't understand that at all.

"She was mean," I said again.

"She's got her burden," Mama said.

She pulled the car back onto the street. It was a long time before she spoke. When we got to Hell's Half Mile, Mama said, "When I was a girl my mama made me some lemonade, put it in a big pitcher, put it on a table out under a tree. She said I should sit there and enjoy it, listen to the birds. So I did. I sat there in a chair in front of the little table and drank my lemonade. I drank it fast. It was sweet. It had so much sugar in it, you had to stir it between glasses, 'cause you didn't, it all settled to the bottom of the pitcher, like sand under water. I drank that pitcher of lemonade so fast because it was so sweet and so good, and then when I got up to go in the house, I was dizzy. It was drinking all that lemonade so fast and it being so sweet. I got real dizzy. I fell when I got to the porch and hit my head on the steps. I still got the scar, just under my hairline. It knocked me out.

"When I come to, Mama had me in the house, stretched out on the couch, and she had bandaged my head. I sat up on the couch when I felt I could, and Mama came in, said, 'You got to learn to take your pleasures slowly, girl. Enjoy them, 'cause there's a lot that isn't pleasurable. And if something is good, and then things go wrong, don't blame the good part if you didn't spend the right kind of time enjoying it.'"

She stopped talking. I thought that was an odd story, considering what had happened that night. As we drove across the Sabine bridge, into Marvel Creek, Mama said, "You see, son, life has got its good and its bad. It's got its lemonade, and it's got blood. Tonight, we had a bit of both. And you can't let the good we did, the lemonade, get outweighed by something that went bad. You got to think slowly on the good, not get caught up in the bad. Got to see the whole picture."

I wasn't sure back then what she was talking about, and by the time we arrived at the house, I had fallen asleep against the car door and had to be shook awake.

8.
IN THE RIVER OF THE DEAD

As we crossed the long Sabine River bridge going out of Marvel Creek, we both turned our heads toward the river, the left side of the bridge. Even from that side we could see the river way out and winding.

I heard Leonard sigh.

I knew what he was remembering. We couldn't drive over the bridge without thinking about it. It was of our first moments together that wasn't just threatening and dangerous, it was deadly.

"That was something," Leonard said, not even bothering to explain what he meant.

"Yeah," I said.

"That's when we were really getting to know each other," he said.

"That's right."

"You did something for me that was damn foolish."

"I did, and I wouldn't do it again."

"Yes, you would. I still have it."

"I know that. By the way, I think it makes a lousy key fob."

"It reminds me of a lot of things, not all of them good," he said. "Sometimes you got to remember the ugly, look it in the eye."

We were across the bridge and out of there, but my memory of what happened wasn't gone, and we sat in silence for a while, both of us remembering it our own way, I guess.

We were seventeen when this happened, out fishing on the Sabine River.

What we learned was if we went fishing, sat in a boat and dragged some lines in the water, we might catch dinner for our night camp, but mostly we found out about each other. That's how I learned about Leonard's family, his feelings about being black and gay, and he learned about my family and me.

We drifted all day, had our camping supplies in the boat, and the plan was we would find a place to stop before nightfall. The boat was pretty good sized, an open boat. The outboard motor wasn't strong on horse power, but it puttered us along as fast as we needed to go.

The river smelled sour because the day was warm. After we motored down a ways, we killed the engine and let the boat drift beneath the shade of the overhanging trees in the narrow part of the river. It was cooler there. The wind finally picked up, which was nice, because it blew the stink and the mosquitoes away from us.

It wasn't quite dark when Leonard snagged his line. Where we were, the Sabine was surprisingly clear. The water ran fast enough we had to drop anchor to keep from floating away. The deep water was so clear, that when Leonard looked to see what his line was snagged on, he saw all the way to the bottom.

"Take a look," he said.

I learned over the side and looked. There was a boat on the bottom.

It wasn't a boat with an outboard. It was one those boats with a top and front and side glasses in the cabin, and it had a real engine. Except for being on the bottom of the river, it looked like a nice boat. Leonard's line had caught up in a side rail, and we could see it clearly. Leonard pulled at the line, but it wouldn't come loose.

"I could swim down there and get it," he said.

"That's deeper than it looks," I said.

"I can swim good," he said. "I'm like fucking Aquaman."

"Just cut the line and go on. Re-rig your tackle."

"I want that sinker," he said.

"A goddamn lead sinker, that's your worry? Shit, I got lead sinkers in my tackle box. Help yourself, and when we get back to shore I'll buy you some more, maybe get you an anvil to tie on your line."

"My uncle gave it to me," he said. "It's made out of lead. It's a little figurine, an old black mammy from some kind of advertisement."

I hadn't noticed he had it. I said, "And you want that?"

"You might not understand it, Hap, but it belongs to my uncle, or did. He gave it to me. It's what we call a keepsake."

"A humiliating little statue made of lead that's a black mammy, and you won't be able to sleep nights if you don't get it? You're jerking my dick?"

"He took it off a man once. A man tried to fight him, made fun of him, and waved that thing under his nose."

"Some guy was carrying it around in his pocket?" I said.

"Story is, my uncle whipped his ass and took that thing and made it his own. Then he gave it to me."

"Try shaking it loose again."

"I've tried," Leonard said. "The hook is under the railing somehow. I'm going to swim down and get it."

"I'll be right here," I said.

Leonard pulled his shirt over his head, slipped off his shoes and pants until he was in his boxer shorts.

Leonard, who had probably seen the same episodes of *Sea Hunt* I had, sat on the edge of the boat and back-flipped into the water. I moved from where I sat and took his former spot, and looked down.

Leonard swam with hard strokes. My guess was right,

it was deeper than it looked. I saw him reach the deck and land on it and pull himself along the railing to where his hook was hung, and I saw his head turn toward the open back door of the boat's cabin. Leonard froze there. He stood there on the deck underwater for a few seconds, and then he forgot the sinker, let go of the railing, and came swimming up hard. I watched him surface like a porpoise and grab the side of the boat. I helped him inside the boat.

"What the fuck?" I said. "You forgot the sinker."

For a black guy he looked a little pale.

"There are bodies down there. Naked bodies."

"What?"

"Bodies."

"What do you mean, bodies?"

"What the fuck do you think I mean, a squirrel and a moose? Fucking bodies. People. I saw a woman and a man floating in there, and they ain't testing the temperature of the water."

"Jesus," I said.

"Yeah, Jesus."

"What do you think happened?"

I thought about it for a moment, stripped off my clothes, and went over the side. The water was cold. When I swam to the deck, I looked through the open door and saw what Leonard had seen. Two bodies. I looked in there, and when I did a child's corpse brushed up against me, made me shoot up to our boat and clamor over the side, almost tipping it.

"There's a child too," I said.

"Shit," Leonard said.

"Yeah. I panicked."

"Me too," Leonard said. "Maybe we should learn not to panic."

"I guess the boat sank fast and they drowned, but damn, couldn't they swim up from that depth? It's deep, but it's not that deep, and the mother or the father could have brought the child up."

"Not if it was so quick they were down there and full of water before they knew it."

"It would have to have had a real blow-out to sink that fast," I said. "I didn't see any rips, so it has to be a hole in the cabin."

"We ought to get someone down here to get them out," Leonard said.

"Yeah," I said. "We got to do that. Look, I'm going down one more time to get your sinker."

"Oh, the hell with it," he said.

"It was everything a few minutes ago, and now it's to hell with it?"

"I hadn't found three dead bodies in a boat then."

I didn't say anything. I was still in my shorts, so I got my pocket knife out of my jeans, opened the knife, and went over the side and swam down. I cut the fishing line loose and got the little lead statue Leonard was using for a sinker and clutched it in my fist. The water was starting to stir and grow dirty, and the sun was going down, laying a strange rust-colored sheen over the water.

I made myself go into the cabin again. It was creepy to see them floating in there, and there was blood too, but it was in odd little strings that floated in the water inside the cabin like odd party confetti.

That kid must have been about four or five years old, and that was a hard thing to see, because when he rolled in the water, which was becoming agitated, I could see there was a hole in his head right over his ear, and when he rolled over, I could see the other side, and there was a larger hole there, one that pretty much replaced that side of his head.

The man and woman were young, and I could see there were burns on their body, and something was stuck up their asses and broken off. Liquor bottles, I thought. There were dark bruises on their necks, and the man's penis had been split down the middle like a banana, and the woman's breasts had burn marks on them. River mud stirred by something washed in and everything turned dark. I panicked and lost my pocket knife and swam up with the lead statue in my fist.

When I topped out of the water, darkness had fallen on the river like a curtain, and it was raining. You couldn't see very far down the river, but you could see a line of rain crossing it and coming in our direction, a rain more fierce than the current one. It was coming in waves and the next wave was going to be rough. The moon wasn't up yet and the stars weren't visible, and with the rain like that, and the clouds, you might not be able to see them anyway.

Leonard pulled me into the boat, and then he got a flashlight and turned it on me. I held out my hand with the statue in it.

"You didn't need to do that, Hap."

"Hell, I know that. Those people, they've been murdered. It's not just a boat drowning."

I told him what I saw.

"Jesus. Well, one thing's for sure. They didn't come out here and do that to themselves, drown their kid and stick bottles up their asses and break them off."

"What I'm saying."

Leonard had already slipped into his clothes, and now I slipped back into mine. They were damp from the rain.

I went to crank the motor, and it wouldn't crank.

Leonard said, "Let me give that a pull."

Any other time I would have turned that line into a joke, but right then I didn't feel too humorous.

He came over and took the rope, and jerked real hard. The rope broke.

"Nice work," I said. "We got to paddle back."

"Tonight? It would take hours. With this rain we won't even be able to see where we're going, and we'll spend all night bailing out the boat."

"But those people," I said.

"Listen, Hap. We got to get the boat on shore, maybe I can screw off the casing on the outboard and figure how to get it going without the rope, or maybe I can tie the rope back together and start it, but it will still be dark and wet as shit. We can dock the boat, spend the night with our camping gear, like we planned to do, and in the morning we can paddle the boat, provided it's not raining like a son-of-a-bitch. And speaking of that."

The rain really hit then. It was heavy and cold and it splattered into the boat and within instants water was starting to rise inside of it.

"So," Leonard said. "A better idea?"

"Let's paddle for shore."

We took the paddles from the bottom of the boat and did just that.

On shore we pulled our supplies from the boat. Our stuff was wrapped in waterproof material inside our packs, so we had that going for us. We placed the packs under a large willow tree that was grouped up with some smaller struggling willows. We tipped the boat to get what water was in it out, and then Leonard used a spare shirt from his pack to rub the boat as dry as he could while I stood over him with a ground cloth stretched over our heads. He didn't completely get out the water, but it helped. I pulled the ground cloth over the top of the boat and tied it around the edges with some fishing line, running the line through gaps in the edges of the boat. The plan was we would sleep in the boat. The idea of sleeping on the ground with water moccasins was highly unappealing.

We needed to eat first, though. We had rain slickers, so we put those on and got up under the willow and used my ground cloth to stretch above us and tie off to limbs to make a kind of rough canopy. Under that we sat against the tree and broke out a can opener and some canned Vienna sausages and Beanee Weenees and ate them with the utensils we had brought, a fork and knife a piece.

"What do you think happened?" I said.

"Well, someone was mad at them for something."

"What could the child have done?"

"Not a thing, I'm sure."

"Maybe the cops can figure it out," I said.

"Maybe they can."

We talked for a long while about it, and then about other things, and then about the boat again. We drank from our canteens. I had some apples in my pack, and got one for both of us. We sat under the tree eating the apples, the rain running off of the ground cloth we had rigged. It was hard to stay dry. It wasn't really a cold night, but with the rain there was a chill, and I wished we had a fire, but the dead wood lying about would be wet, and we decided it wasn't worth gathering it and decided to keep a cold camp.

Our plan was to get under the canopy in the boat, and with our flashlights, read. We had brought books for just that plan, but the truth was neither of us felt like reading or going to sleep. Every time we stopped talking, I saw in my head that poor child and those people, brutalized, down there in the water with fish swimming amongst them, not to mention snakes and what have you. It wasn't a good image.

"What about our motor?" I said.

"In the morning. I can't see shit in this rain."

"Those poor people," I said.

"They won't get any deader," Leonard said. "We'll head back in the morning."

"Sure," I said.

"We ought to go to bed."

"Yeah."

But we didn't.

"In the morning, we'll find enough dry wood to make some coffee," Leonard said.

"If you brought coffee. I got a pot we can cook it in, strain the grounds through something, but I don't have any coffee."

"I thought you said you would bring the coffee?"

"No. I said we needed coffee."

"You said that, I thought you meant you better get some."

"Nope. I just wanted some. I thought you were going to bring it."

"Perfect."

That's when we heard a motor on the river and saw a boat with a strong forward light coming upriver. We sat silent and watched it slow down, then go by where we were. A little later we heard it turning back and saw the light again as the boat came back in our direction.

"I think they're looking for the boat?" Leonard said.

"You think they know where it is?"

"Yeah."

"Why?"

"A guess."

The boat passed our camp again, but didn't go far before it turned around and they brought the boat alongside the bank and not far from the tree where we were. Leonard took out his pocket knife and opened it. I had lost my knife. I sat there with wishful thinking and no weapon.

The boat on the water was not too unlike the boat on the bottom of the river, and there were at least three men on it. I could hear them talking, though I couldn't hear what they were saying. They were still inside the cabin, but the door to the cabin was open, and their voices came out along with some light. In a little while they walked out on deck.

They had on hooded rain slickers. They were on the far side of their boat, away from shore, leaning over with their lights pointed at the water.

"Can't see a damn thing," one of the men said. He was the largest of the three.

"This is the place," said another, who was a shorter version of the biggest man.

"You sure?" said the big man.

"Pretty sure."

The third man, a thin guy, said, "You better be sure. That water is going to be cold, and it's going to be you going in."

The shorter stocky man at the side of the boat, leaning over the railing, stood up, said, "I'm not the only one going in, not in this dark water. I go, we all go, or we wait until morning."

There was a silence on the boat, and then the biggest of the three, a fellow who seemed in charge, said, "Alright. We stay until morning, then we go in. Maybe the rain will be done."

"It will be," said the thinner man.

"How the hell would you know?" said the short stocky one.

"You get so you know one kind of rain from another. This one is hard for a while, and then it'll move on. Might be some light rain later, but when this is gone, it'll gradually start to clear."

"Listen to Farmer Brown," said the short stocky man. "We grew up with him, but he's got some special skills given to him by the angels or some such."

"We'll stay in the cabin until daylight," said the big man, "then we go in."

They were all standing together now, looking at the shore line. The one that knew about farming said, "There's a boat on shore."

"So what," said the big man. "People leave them here all the time to go fishing. Lots of niggers live on this stretch, back beyond the tree stand. Probably one of their boats."

Without saying a thing to one another, me and Leonard both stretched out and lay flat on the ground behind the big willow and the scrubs. We tried to make ourselves as small as possible.

The head man studied where we were for a while, then shined his light on us. He could pick up on Leonard real good.

He said, "There's a nigger lying down there."

"Run for it, to the left. I'll go right," Leonard said, lying in the pool of light. "They ain't seen you yet."

By this time the short stocky man had slipped into the cabin, and he came out with a rifle. He pointed it at the shore where Leonard lay.

"Better come out of there, nigger, or I'm gonna pop you," said the short stocky man. "You can't run faster than a bullet."

Leonard stood up and dropped his knife on the ground. "I'm just out here fishing."

"Are you now?"

The thinner's man's flashlight came on and the beam fell on me. "There's another one on the other side. White boy."

I stood up slowly. I thought I probably could make a run for it, as the grass and brush was high on my side, and there were some trees a little farther down, and it would be hard for them to get a clear shot. But I couldn't leave Leonard.

Since their boat was close to shore, the man with the rifle jumped down and came over. He walked on the edge of the flashlight beam that was shining on Leonard. The other man kept his light on me. It was a strong light. I felt like I was part of a floor show.

When they were all three on shore, the big man said, "Fishing, huh?"

"That's right," I said. "Our motor broke down, and there came a rain storm, so we put in for the night."

"Cheap ass motor is my guess," said the one with the gun.

"I reckon that's true," Leonard said.

"You seen us looking over the side of our boat, didn't you?" said the head man.

"Sure, we seen you," Leonard said. "What you looking for?"

"Nothing that concerns you, nigger. Both of you, come down here closer on the bank."

Leonard led the way and I followed up. I was starting to regret the both of us not trying to make a break for it.

The big man put his light in our faces, stared at us while we blinked.

"You know what's down there, don't you?" he said. "I can tell when someone has a secret, and I can guess at it damn good, know what that secret is. Been able to do that all my life."

"Another one of us with special powers," said the man with the rifle.

"What are you talking about?" I said.

"The boat," the big man said.

"Shit, August, don't tell him." said the man with the gun.

"Hell, they already know. I can tell by looking at them. They know why we're here."

"Haven't a clue," Leonard said.

"I know a liar when I hear one," the big man said, the one called August.

"We'll have to kill them," said the one with the rifle. "They didn't know, they know now, way you've run your mouth."

The big man glanced at the one with the rifle, and the rifle man went silent. I think he knew there was a line he shouldn't cross with the big man.

I thought: Shit, this is it. I'm going to die on the banks of the Sabine River, and here I was close to graduation and hoping I was going out into a wider world away from all these crackers, but instead I was going to die at their hands.

Typical.

"Can you boys swim?" August said.

"Like a goddamn eel," Leonard said.

"You?" he said, indicating me, of course.

"Yes."

August contemplated for a few moments, said, "What I'm thinking, is we have them swim down for us, have them get it, and we don't have to get cold and wet and take a chance down there. Just the thought of my balls in that cold water makes me ill."

"Only need one of them," the man with the rifle said. "We could pop the nigger."

"Naw, it's heavy," August said. "We need them both."

I knew another sentence had stayed inside his head. And it went like this: "And then we pop them both."

They brought us on the boat and had us sit down on the deck. The deck was wet and I could feel it through my pants. It made my ass cold. Now that they weren't shining the lights right on us, I could actually see them better. August was the biggest, and I took him for the planner. He had a way of leaning forward all the time, as if he was about to take off in a sprint. He was too big a man to get far that way, I judged, but he was certainly the right size for twisting your head off. The man with the rifle, the leanest of the three, had a nervousness that made me nervous. I didn't like the way he handled the gun. His hair was cut short like the other two, so short I figured they might as well just go on and shave their heads. All three looked kin. Brothers or cousins perhaps, the thin one being the most different in size, but not in facial features.

"There's some dead people down there in a boat," said August, "but you know that. I can tell by looking at you. But what you might not know is they're there for a reason. They been hauling off stuff that isn't theirs."

"Yeah," said the one with the rifle. "They fucked up."

"What kind of stuff?" I asked.

"They don't need to know shit," said the one with the rifle.

"It's alright, Tom. I want to tell them. Besides, they knew the bodies were there, I promise you. Come on, admit, you knew they were there."

We said nothing.

"That's alright," August said. "I'm going to tell you all about it."

"Why the hell should you?" Tom said.

"Know what they're looking for, that's why."

"You don't have to tell them why, just what it looks like," Tom said.

"I know that," August said.

I could tell August was the kind of guy that wanted to brag on himself, thought he was a real top cat and wanted everyone to know it. I thought of a line Tony Curtis had in movie, a line about wanting to be Charlie Potatoes, meaning the big man. That was this guy. He knew too it didn't matter what he told us. Later on we'd be in the river with the other three.

"What do you think it is down there?" August asked us.

"Your mother's china," Leonard said.

"Oh, nigger, you are not in a position to crack wise," August said.

"Just making a guess," Leonard said.

I had learned that Leonard, under the direst of times, couldn't help himself with the smart remark. I'm not much better. I think it was the way we coped with intense stress, and maybe in Leonard's case he just didn't give a shit. I, on the other hand, gave a big shit, and didn't want to end up with a bullet in my head with my body absorbing river water.

"That isn't any guess. Them three down there, that's

the Smiths. What they called themselves anyway. You can call them dead now. Thought they were going to be clever. Said they'd buy some smack from us, that they'd come to our place by boat, on account of we live on the river."

"Best reason to come by boat," Leonard said.

"What?" said August.

"If you didn't live on the river, then they'd come by car, maybe airplane."

"Keep it up, coon. Keep it up."

"Shut up," Tom said. "They don't need to know any of this shit."

"I like telling it," August said.

August picked up where he left off. It was easy to see that telling us what a smart and bad motherfucker he was gave him great pleasure. The other two could care less, and we were a new audience. It gave him a reason to hear himself talk.

"Smiths had it in their mind they were going to rob us and take the dope, sell it to hippies some place. Dallas. Austin. Shit, I don't know, San Francisco. They talked like Yankees, so I don't know. But they been in this area for a while, and they been buying, a bit here and there, and I guess they were storing it up, going to resell it up north, and they heard about us. We met them at the feed store, and they said they had the money and we said we had the dope. So we made a deal.

"Know what they did?"

"You already told us," Leonard said. "They robbed you."

This didn't deter August.

"They came down the river in their boat. They had guns. We did too, but they surprised us. Nice looking couple, and they had that kid with them. Quiet kid. Either trained to keep his mouth shut or quiet by nature."

"Would have been nice had you been that way," Tom said.

August ignored him.

"I figure they thought it made them look normal, going down the road in a van pulling a boat loaded with dope, 'cause no one would think to look at them for such a thing. Shit, we were going to rob them and they outfoxed us and got the jump on us. So they got our stash. It's wrapped in plastic and duct taped and in a cooler that's taped, and they took off with it. They had us open it up, show what was in it while they held guns on us, then they had us tape and fasten it all up, load it on their boat, but, you see, they fucked up. They should have wrecked our boat, 'cause soon as they left we went after them. We got a better and faster boat. We caught up with them back river a ways. You know what we did to really hurt them? We shot that fucking kid right in the head. First thing. *Bam.* That made them scream, it truly did, didn't it, Tom?"

Tom nodded, said, "They shouldn't have put us in that position."

"That's right," August said. "They put us there. Then we had some fun with the woman and we gave them a bit of a lesson with fire and such, shot them in the head.

But you know what happened? I don't even think they knew it. They had gone over some shallows and hit some rocks, and it took the bottom of their boat out, and it sunk with them on it, and us having to swim back to our boat right when we were about to bring the dope out. When it started going down, it went down fast as a fucking torpedo."

"It was already going down," said Tom, "but no one noticed. We were all busy."

"That's right," August said. "But then we're done with them and there's water on our feet, and down the boat goes, and by this time it's night, and we decided we'd wait until the morning. You see, we got their money back, but they had our dope. We figured going down in that water at night . . . Well, we didn't know how deep it was, but we knew that boat sunk like a fucking stone. We knew too, come the next day we could check it out. We marked the place and went on home. Next day the sheriff, who I might add is running for election, which means he needs a good drug bust or catching someone peddling pussy to raise his profile, came around. We got a kind of rep for things the cops don't like, so he chooses us, comes sniffing around our place with a warrant, having heard something from somebody about this or that. Thin evidence."

"But they were right," said Tom. "We were selling dope. It's bigger money than pussy. Guy gets dope, likes it, pretty soon he can't think about pussy anymore. He thinks about dope. And women, they like that dope just fine too. Like it good as anybody."

"Tom, shut up, I'm telling this. So there we were all day while the county turned over row boats, looked through this boat, searched our house and the sheds. They looked everywhere but up the dog's ass. It took them some time to do it, but they didn't find anything. All our dope was in that boat at the bottom of the river. Our family business with that goddamn family, and in a way they done us a favor. They took with them what would have gotten our dicks in a crack. We had just put it out for show, to get their money, and then they took it, and it worked out fine.

"So here were are, come to get the dope, and guess the fuck what? After all that shit with the cops, us waiting until they had their hands out of our pants, well, it's night again. We brought some good lights, some underwater lights, and we thought we might go down and get it, but decided to just stay here until morning. Then we found you two. You're like an answer to a fucking prayer, that's what you are. You know what I'm thinking?"

"Yeah," Leonard said. "With us here, why wait until daybreak?"

"Now you got it. You know, you're a pretty smart nigger."

"I'll tell my teachers," Leonard said.

"What's it look like, Jaret?" August asked, and now we knew the other guy's name.

128

"Like water," Jaret said.

"Come on, goddamnit," August said.

"It ain't as muddy as a bit ago," Jaret said. "It ain't clear, but it ain't all that muddy either."

"So you're going to send us down there to get something out of a boat we can't even see?" Leonard said.

Tom looked out at the water. "It's stopped raining and the water is running fast. My guess is it'll clear up some more in an hour or so."

August studied us. "Well, boys, you got some time to sit there and think. You want to pull your dicks, or one another's dick, then now's the time."

He laughed at his own joke.

I studied the man with the gun. He was our main worry, but those other two were big guys, especially August, and from the looks of them, they'd been in a few brawls.

We kept sitting, and August kept talking. He was like a chatter box on speed. He just wouldn't shut up. And then I got it. He was on speed.

August talked about himself. He talked about his family, and during the conversation it was made certain that those two guys were his brothers. He talked about his old man, and how he was working under a car on a creeper, just his legs sticking out, and how he had gotten killed when the jack holding up the car slipped and the car dropped and crushed him. Tom laughed when August told that story. It got funnier for Tom when August talked about the reason the jack slipped. August said he kicked the jack loose holding up the car and when it fell on his father it made a squishing sound and shit ran out of his father's pants leg. Then there was a pool of piss and blood that oozed out from under the car along with the shit.

"Ah hell, we don't know you actually kicked that jack," Jaret said. "It could have slipped."

"I kicked it," said August.

"If you say so," said Jaret. "I don't think you had the balls for that."

"You think what you want," August said.

This bothered August enough for him to go quiet for a while, but alas, it didn't last. He started talking again.

"Old man disrespected our mother once too often," August said. "I had to take him out. Also, he beat our asses all the time. Mine especially. I think he liked how that belt sounded against my back or upside my head. I got a scar over my right ear where he hit me with the buckle. Had more light, I'd show it to you."

"I don't care to see your scars," Leonard said.

August by now was ignoring Leonard. He had stories to tell and he was going to tell them if we were interested or not. He told us about a calf he used to get behind, climb up on a stump, and fuck. He talked about that calf like it was a long lost girlfriend. I kept thinking a prom story would come up next. He told how the calf became a cow and he had to take a step stool out to the pasture to fuck it after a time because its ass got tall. Told us how once when he was laying the meat into it, his words, the cow shit and filled his pants, and how this happened one morning right before school and the school bus was coming, and there he was with pants full of shit.

He seemed to think that was a natural and funny thing.

Later, he and the family ate the girlfriend.

"Old man, before he was crushed, of course," August said, as if we might not put that together, "used to say you got to break them calves in early on account of once the bull gets to them they get stretched out like sweat pants."

And so it went. We learned everything about August but his shoe size, and I think that was coming, but Jaret said, "It's pretty clear now. With a light, I think they can see what they're doing."

"Yeah," Tom said. "We got some diver's masks in there and you can wear them. We were going to."

"You still can," Leonard said.

"No," Tom said, "we got you. You drown or a gator eats you or a snake bites you, it don't mean shit to us. But if we drown, that means a big shit."

"Not to us," Leonard said.

"I figure that's right," said Tom

"But no diver's gear other than a mask?" I said, as if I had any idea how to use diver's gear, but the idea of air tanks was appealing.

"The masks," said Tom. "That's it. Hope you can hold your breath good."

"Let me get this straight," Leonard said. "We go down there and get your dope, come back up, you're going to let us go?"

"Sure," August said.

"I don't know that I believe that," Leonard said.

"It don't matter what you believe," August said. "We plan to kill you, at least this way you got a little longer to stay alive, and you come up with our goods, who the fuck knows? Might feel happy enough to let you go. If not, well, you had a refreshing swim, didn't you?"

They washed the masks in the water so they would stick to our faces better and gave them to us. We put them on and went over and stood by the side of the boat like they said. We took off our clothes, like they said, stripped down to our shorts. We stood near naked in the chill night air and the harsh light that August was pointing at us.

"Here's what you do," Tom said. "You swim down there, and you go in the cabin, where the bodies are, and you look to the right, and there's a built-in wall chest there. They had the dope there, and we left it there while we did what we did with them, and then the goddamn boat sunk. You get it out of that and bring it up. Probably take both of you. Swim it up and give it to us and we'll let you go. You don't even have to get back in the boat. We'll let you swim off."

"And take this with you," August said.

He went inside the cabin and came out with a big handheld underwater light. "Use this, you can see better."

He handed me the light.

"And if it's too muddy to see even with the light?" Leonard said.

"You better hope you can feel your way, because you come up without that dope, we're going to shoot a hole in you."

"They might have to go down a couple times, find it, come back for a breath and get it," Jaret said. "We could tie a rope off here, let them take it down and tie it to the boat. That would give them a line to follow when they come up, make things quicker and easier."

"Guess that's right," August said, and rubbed under his nose. "So, okay. You get to come up once, maybe twice, but third time better be the fucking charm, or just stay down there and drown."

August looped one end of the rope through the boat's railing and gave the length of rope to Leonard.

I glanced at Leonard. He gave me a smile thin as the edge of a switchblade.

We took deep breaths and went over the side.

It was like being inside a cloud, the mud was so thick, but we kept swimming down, close together because I had the light. Finally we swam under the mud and it was a lot clearer. Not like it had been before when we first found them, but you could make out things pretty good.

Something heavy bumped into me, and I twisted away from it, and even in the grimy underwater light, I could see it was the child. He had come free of the open cabin door and was floating about in the river. It was eerie seeing him swirling around there, and the water kept shoving him at me, and when he touched me it felt like rubber. I pushed the little body away from me and that's when Leonard grabbed my shoulder.

I turned and looked at him. He was right in front of my face. He raised his hand and pointed down. I got it together and shined the light down and swam after the beam. Below we saw the boat, the cabin rising up, and the grasses and vines on the bottom of the river were swirling around. It wasn't like when we were down there in daytime. It was like an underwater haunted house.

The river was running fast and it was hard to swim in it, but it was easier the lower we got, another couple of feet down and it was totally different, calm almost. I was glad we got to the boat, but I was starting to lose my breath and knew I had to pop up pretty soon.

Leonard looked as if he was doing okay. He tied his end of the rope off on the boat's railing, and then he was swimming inside the cabin, and I swam after him. The man and woman were twisting about in the murky light, bumping against one another and against the walls and the glass of the cabin, like they were doing some kind of macabre dance.

It was all I could do to not focus on them.

We found the built-in chest, and Leonard tugged at

it, but it was staying in place. I went over and hung the light on a wall hook for jackets. The light shone down on the chest. I helped Leonard tug at it. We fought at it, trying to open it for a while, and then I patted him on the shoulder and pointed up.

Leonard nodded.

I took the light off the hook, went out of the cabin, and started following the rope up. When we broke the surface, all three of them were leaning over looking at us. I let the line shine in their eyes a moment until one of them cursed, and then I pulled it away from them and held onto it. I pushed my mask up.

"Well, where the fuck is it?" August said.

"Still down there," I said.

"Why is that?"

"Because we ran out of breath, and opening the chest underwater isn't that easy."

"That sounds like a personal problem," Tom said.

"Be that as it may, it's fastened tight," I said.

"We need a hatchet, or a knife, or something to pry up the chest, or break it open," Leonard said.

"Why would I give you assholes a hatchet?" August said.

"I just told you," Leonard said.

"Hell, give it to them," Jaret said. "Tom's got the rifle."

August stood there looking at us hanging on the rope, then went away and came back with a machete that had a little leather loop for hanging on the wrist or on a belt. It was in a green, canvas scabbard, and he pulled it out of the scabbard and handed it to Leonard.

"Take this, and goddamnit, don't cut the cooler open. Don't break it apart or the water will ruin it."

"Got it," I said.

"It gets ruined, you get shot," August said.

"We might need to come up once more for air," Leonard said. "It takes it out of you. The current is strong and it wears you out to tug on that goddamn chest lid."

"You come up a third time and you don't have that chest," August said, "I shoot you, and we wait until morning and clear water and get it ourselves."

Tom pointed the rifle at us. "I'm thinking one of you, with a little work, could pull that chest up. I don't like there's two of you out there."

"It takes two," Leonard said. "Listen fellows, all we want to do is swim down and get it and bring it up so you can let us go."

Tom pulled a face, said, "Alright. Get on with it."

Down we went again, this time following the rope Leonard had fastened, me with the light and Leonard with the machete. It was a lot quicker using the rope as a guide, pulling ourselves down it instead of swimming all the way.

We got to the boat and with a lot of work we worked the wall chest open, and there was the ice chest inside, wrapped up in duct tape. First thing Leonard did was he took the machete and cut the tape loose with a few slices, and then he got the lid open by prying it with the machete, and then he stabbed into the wrapped bags inside. The dope came out in a white cloud, and I figured fish would be dying, or a week from now begging another hit. Water moccasins would be swimming in formation, conducting a water ballet. I pushed back from the stuff. It all went up to the top of the cabin and floated there, then slowly the cloud spread and it eased out of the open doorway as if it were a living thing.

Leonard let the machete dangle off his wrist by the thong, and then we swam out of the cabin, Leonard taking the lead. We kept swimming close to the bottom, kept at it until I thought my lungs would burst and I was starting to feel dizzy. Leonard got up close to me and took the light from me and pointed it and we swam where he pointed the beam. Finally we started rising up because we needed air. As we rose through a cloud of silt, Leonard cut the light and let go of it. I felt it bump my leg as it went down.

Sudden loss of the light turned the river black as compost, but we kept rising up, and then there was a pattern in the water made by moonlight and tree shadow. It was like a camouflage netting had been tossed over the surface of the river. We broke the water lightly, just our heads above it, pushed our masks up, and looked back. We could see the boat sitting in its spot, the three dumb asses leaning over the side, looking down. The boat lights gave us a view of the heroin rising to the surface in a white foam all around the boat, and then the foam subsided and the river began to darken again.

I heard August scream, "Goddamnit."

I was hoping they thought we had drowned, dropped the ice chest and it had busted open. Leonard touched my shoulder, nodded toward the riverbank.

We swam as silently as we could and came to a series of old stumps in the water. The land and its dead tree stumps had been claimed by the river over time, but it was shallow there, and as we made our way to shore it was hard to be silent. I expected them to hear us splashing about and bullets would crash into us before we made the riverbank.

The clouds were gone now and the moon was bright. Tendrils of light twisted in through the trees like silver gauze. With our skin still wet it was cool out of the water, and though it was not a winter night, there was a breeze, and it was steady. We worked our way deeper into the tree line.

My feet hurt from all the pokes it got from forest debris, and I figured what might be an end to a perfect night was to be snake bit or scorpion stung, if not shot in the back of the head, but we managed to finally get deep into the trees. The wind was less cool there. We tossed the face masks and started moving more quickly. Once we surprised a possum. It hissed and made me jump three feet back, but it rustled into the greenery and out of sight, looking there in the mottled moonlight like a giant rat.

We stopped to whisper to one another for a while,

figuring what to do next, decided we would find a spot in the trees where we could see the river and their boat. When we made that spot, we saw Tom hand his rifle to August, and then he started taking his clothes off. He stripped completely naked and eased over the side where the rope was, and then we couldn't see him anymore.

Squatting there in the woods, looking through gaps in low-hanging limbs and splits in thick-leafed brush, a lot of time passed. We trembled in the cool breeze. It was obvious August and Jaret were starting to get worried. They paced the deck. Finally, Jaret stripped down and went over the side.

I don't know how much time passed, couple of minutes maybe, before Jaret came up. His head rose over the edge of the boat as he pulled himself inside, then he and August started pulling on the rope. After some time they bent down over the side and hoisted Tom's body into the boat. It flopped on the deck like a big, white fish.

I got it then. Tom had gone down to see if there was some dope to be saved. He followed the rope, but we had the big light, and he got confused, trapped in the cabin and couldn't get out. Something like that. Jaret had groped around down there and found him and found the rope again, unfastened it and tied Tom's body to it, and came up by the rope. Then he and August had pulled Tom up.

There came a sob so loud and sad from August, that even under the circumstances I felt his pain. Jaret kept saying over and over, "Those goddamn bastards.

Goddamnit. We should have shot them soon as we seen them."

Leonard said, "Ha, the fucker drowned."

I was learning Leonard was short on sympathy for assholes.

They were there for a while, crying and bawling like children, and all that did was make Leonard snicker. I on the other hand felt damn bad about it, but wasn't sure why. They would have killed us as easily as looking at us if we had brought that dope chest up. Maybe even tortured us like they did the family, just because they could. All in all, we had turned out alright, not dead, not in the depths of the river with bottles stuck up our asses.

I don't know how long we shivered there, but eventually August went inside the cabin with Jaret. The boat motor fired up, lights came on, and the boat made a loop in the river and started back the way it came.

We eased down to our camp site then, got spare clothes out of our packs and got dressed. Neither of us had spare shoes. The only way back to Marvel Creek was by river, and that meant we had to go the way they had gone.

I don't know how long we waited, but it was a long time. We didn't want to wait until daylight, because if we came upon them they would be sure to see us, but we were hoping to give them enough time to get off the river and pass wherever they were in the night. From the way they talked, they lived right along the bank.

Leonard had me hold the flashlight while he took the little tool kit he had, and slipped the motor cover off. He messed with it awhile, but couldn't do anything with it. If we went back to Marvel Creek we'd be paddling upriver for hours, and I wasn't sure we could do it, fight the current all night. And still there was that whole thing about maybe being seen passing wherever they lived. Hell, they might even be looking for us.

We put our supplies back in the boat, slid the boat down to the river. The river carried us along with its flow, away from the way we had come, and we let it, using our paddles to speed up the process. It was a safer way to go, but it was going to be a while before we came to any place that was worth stopping.

Day eased away the night, and the water lit up with sunrise and was rust-colored, then within minutes, it turned dark brown. The air was cool with wind for a while, but it wasn't long before it turned still and hot. We paddled onward.

There were fishing camps along the way, but we didn't stop to talk to anyone there, as we couldn't be certain who those three knew along the river. At some point someone took a shot at us, and we paddled really hard. No more shots came.

Eventually we came to a clearing off to our left, and we paddled for that, pulled the boat on shore, then sat back down in it to rest. We hadn't been there long when we heard an engine groaning, and all of a sudden a black pickup barreled up beside us. It was going so fast I thought it would go into the river, but it didn't. The truck braked and the doors slammed and two young men got out. I thought, okay, now what the fuck?

They came down and saw us sitting there in the boat.

"You have to put it in the water, you want to go anywhere," said one of the boys. He was blond and stocky and had a little bit of blond fuzz on his chin that looked so thin you got the impression he could have wiped it off with a rag. The other was a darker-haired boy with a five o'clock shadow at the break of day.

"We've just stopped for a while," I said.

The blond boy nodded. "Fishing?"

"Have been," Leonard said. "Didn't catch a thing."

"You ain't got no shoes?" said the dark-haired boy.

"We just ain't wearing any," Leonard said.

The dark-haired boy nodded. "I got some nigger friends" he said.

"That's nice," Leonard said. "I got some cracker buddies." He pointed at me. "There's one now."

This made them laugh out loud. I was glad for that. I wasn't sure they were the humorous type, but turned out they were. I had yet to determine which direction that humor could go.

The blond said, "Shit, man, I took a shot at you guys earlier."

"Oh," I said. "That was you?"

I thought it was about to all go south, end up with us

being shot and butt-fucked while dead.

"Yeah," said the blond. "I thought you was my brother."

"Ah," I said. I didn't examine that comment any further. I merely said, "Is there a town nearby? Our boat motor played out, and we thought we might get it fixed."

"What's wrong with it?" the blond said.

"It don't work," Leonard said.

The blond laughed. "You're a hoot. I always say, you want to laugh, hang with niggers."

"That's why we black folks are here, to make you laugh," Leonard said.

The blond boy studied Leonard for a moment. "I like you."

"I'm glad," Leonard said.

"Let's look at that motor," the blond said. "Leroy, look at the fucker." Then to us, "Leroy could fix the dead Jesus."

Leroy went back to the pickup, leaned into the bed and pulled out a toolbox. We got out of the boat and he got in. He popped the sheath off the motor and pottered around a bit, poking it with a screw driver, and after a while he popped it with a hammer a bit, then took a wrench to it. Within fifteen minutes he had pulled the rope out of where it had disappeared, and he managed to get enough of it to go back through the gap in the sheath after he put that back on. He tied the end of the rope over the handle of the hammer, and let that clamp up against the gap. Then he used the bit of rope with the pull handle lying in the boat to fasten it back together with the rope he had saved, freeing his hammer and making a big knot so it wouldn't slip back through the gap.

"You ain't got as much pull room," said the dark-haired boy, "but it ought to go now."

"Thanks," I said. "I haven't got any money to give you, but if you want my fishing tackle, you can have that."

"Naw," said the blond boy. "You'll need that. We don't fish much anyway. We come down here to shoot turtles mostly. We can help you push the boat in the water, you're ready to go."

"We are," I said.

They helped us get the boat back in the water, and as we were climbing in, the dark-haired boy said, "You fellows want a beer? We got some cold ones."

"I'm going to pass," I said.

"Sure," Leonard said. "I'll have a beer, and I wouldn't fight you off if you offered me a pretzel."

The blond laughed. "You niggers are funny."

"What we black folk tell ourselves all the time," Leonard said.

"Y'all really do that?" said the blond boy.

"Naw," Leonard said. "I'm just fucking with you."

That made both boys laugh. The dark-haired one brought Leonard a beer from the truck, handed it to him without him having to get out of the boat. I used my paddle to push off.

"Thanks again," I said.

"Sure," said the blond.

"Don't shoot at us no more," I said.

"Naw. I thought I was fucking with my brother."

Leonard pulled the rope on the motor and the motor caught and away we went.

Eventually we turned the boat around and headed to Marvel Creek. We weren't as scared with a motor to speed us on. Nobody shot at us again, and we didn't see August and Jaret. When we got back to Leonard's truck and fastened the boat on the boat rack, I used the pay phone outside the feed store to call the cops. I told them about what we had found. I told them about August, Jaret, and Tom. I told them about the bodies in the boat and about the dope. I gave them a kind of overview of all that had happened, and did my best to indicate where the sunken boat was. I didn't give our names. I didn't want to be pulled into it. I didn't trust how the law would take our presence. They might think we were a part of the whole thing.

We went home after that, and the next day I read in the local paper how the Robbie family, which was the first time I'd heard their last name, had been arrested for murder, and how the law found Tom's body on their property. They were digging a hole out behind the house to bury him when the law came up with a search warrant. Eventually the Robbie boys, perhaps with the persuasion of rubber hoses and phone books upside the head, admitted they had killed the family, and showed the law where the sunken boat was. Of course, there was no more dope. The man's and the woman's bodies were claimed, but they didn't find the child.

About a week before Christmas I read in the paper that the kid's remains were found caught up in some stumps and brush. There wasn't much left of him by then, of course, but it was the child alright.

The little black mammy figurine, which was about the size of a chess piece, quit being one of Leonard's fishing sinkers. He fastened it to his key chain, and when he gets a new ride, he always moves the figurine to his latest set of keys.

Sometimes, I lay down at night, and there, in the dark of my dreams, swirling around and around, is that poor unfortunate child, his head blown apart. It's a dream that's been with me so long, I can from time to time wish him back into a swirling cloud of shadow, push him and the knowledge of what some people can do to others, far away from me.

9.
STOPPING FOR COFFEE

We tooled back to my house. Brett and Chance and Buffy were home. The car was parked in its spot in the car port.

When we came in Brett was at the table playing checkers with Chance. Our shepard, Buffy, was lying under the table, her head on Chance's foot.

"Who's winning?"

"Brett is," Chance said. "I thought I had her a couple of times, but she blindsided me."

"She cheats a little," I said.

"Do not," Brett said, lifting her head so quick her thick mane of red hair snapped up and the clasp on it came loose and her hair cascaded over her shoulders like a fiery waterfall. "Now look what you made me do."

"This," Leonard said, "is when you grab a checker, when she's picking up a hair tie, or push one closer."

"Not likely," Brett said. "I memorize the board."

"She does, you know," Chance said.

Chance, my daughter, was just the opposite of Brett. She was dark skinned, with dark eyes and hair as deeply dark as the bottom of a coal mine. They were both lovely. They were both wearing footy pajamas and had cups of hot chocolate near the board.

"How was the club?"

"Kasey was good," Chance said. "We hung out a little after she got offstage. I got my CD signed. The food there was lousy."

"How was Buffy?" I said.

"She was okay. I think toward the end she just wanted a place to crap and then lie down," Brett said. "The noise and the crowd made her nervous."

"Were there a lot of dogs?" Leonard said.

"A few. It doesn't work as well as you might think. The dogs get nervous with all the noise. I give it another six months, and then that place closes."

"Is there any more hot chocolate?" I said.

"If you make it," Brett said.

"Oh," I said.

"Vanilla cookies?" Leonard asked.

"Nope," Brett said.

"Animal crackers, though," Chance said. "In the cabinet by the sink."

I opened the cabinet and got out a large canister of animal crackers. My mouth was already watering.

"Those would be nice with chocolate," Leonard said. "I mean, if any was made."

"Wouldn't they?" I said. "Oh, okay. I'll make us some. But stay out of the animal crackers until I do."

I heated up some chocolate and poured us cups and we sat at the table with the ladies. They had wrapped up their game and Brett was folding up the checker board and gathering up the checkers and slipping them into the box.

"So, you boys been playing?" Brett said.

"Some," I said. "We punched each other and rode around for a while."

"Did you and Leonard do this when you were kids?" Chance said. "Drink chocolate and eat animal crackers?"

"We didn't meet until we were seventeen," I said. "And had we met before then, might not have been so easy to hang out."

"Oh, yeah, of course," Chance said. "I forgot. My history is shorter. How bad was it then?" she asked.

"Darling," Leonard said. "You don't want to know."

"I don't know things are all that better," Brett said.

"Oh hell, sure they are," Leonard said. "They got a ways to go, but they are nothing like they used to be. Let me tell you, those times blew. Me and Hap grew up in a racist, mean-spirited time, and I have never been one to say race has held me back, nor has being a homo, but it was worse then, at least in those respects."

"Still a lot underground, though," I said.

"Shit," Brett said. "It's not all that underground. Last few years, they're surfacing like dead bodies floating up. It's actually the change that's scaring the mean-spirited.

The idea that it won't be like it used to be, even if it was never like they think it was, drives them crazy."

"On the same page," I said.

"Yeah, you're right," Leonard said. "But now I get to go in a store and buy a Coke and not have people looking at me. I can sit down in a restaurant and eat. I was a boy, couldn't do that. Neither could my uncle, and he wasn't happy about it. He caused a few scenes. Amazing he lived long as he did. He bucked that system. Being a homo wasn't all that easy for me either. For the dumb asses, being gay was the same as being a child molester. Didn't matter that child molesters come from both sides of the fence, you got labeled that, like all we did was hang around bus stop restrooms waiting to snatch a child and carry them into a stall in the toilet. I pushed forward no matter what. I think it made me stronger, it being like that and me going up against it."

"I think it was an unnecessary barrier and a burden," I said. "But you're right. It was worse, though if some people have their way, it'll go back to the dark ages."

"Sounds horrible," Chance said.

"Give Chance a history lesson," Leonard said. "Tell her about the café."

It was something Leonard knew about, but neither Brett nor Chance did. I didn't like talking about it. Didn't like thinking about it. But . . .

"Yeah," I said, "you ought to know. Ought to understand how things were, how they've changed, and how we don't want them to slip back into that old groove. Not in any kind of way."

Chance gained a serious look. "What happened, Daddy?"

On that afternoon I was out driving. I was sixteen and had owned my license for only a short time. I was going from LaBorde to Tyler, not for any reason, but just because I could. I had tried to find someone to ride with me, a girl hopefully, but I hadn't had any luck, so I went on my own.

It was a nice day at first, but then it got cloudy and started to rain. I hadn't planned to stop at the café, but the rain seemed to have come out of nowhere and it was very serious. By the time I reached No Enterprise, a place about a third of the way between LaBorde and Tyler, the wipers on my '64 Chevy Impala were working hard and accomplishing little. The ditches and gullies in the town were rolling with water and the water was flooding over them and into the street. I could barely see what was in front of me. I did manage to see some lights through the rain, off to the left, and when I felt I could safely cross the road, I did, and pulled in where the lights were. It was a café.

I decided to wait out the rain. I sat in the car to do it, and then I thought, well, if I'm going to wait I might as well go inside and have some coffee. The idea of being able to go inside and do that somehow made me feel like an adult. I had never really done that before, driven along by myself and stopped somewhere to have coffee on my own. It sounds like a little thing, but right then I thought it was a swell and amazing idea.

Jumping out of the car, I ran inside, shedding water and wiping my feet at the door. The place smelled of hamburgers, the way they only could smell back then when I was a kid and they were cooked on old black grills that were never truly cleaned by anything other than heat and scraping off the grease with a spatula.

I went in and sat down at a booth on the side and waited for my waitress. There were three older men sitting at a table, and two guys I judged to be in their thirties at a booth near the kitchen.

The waitress, an older woman with a slight limp and badly dyed hair that made it look blue, came over and asked me what I wanted. I told her coffee, but by then I had added a hamburger to the order and some French fries. Those burgers cooking really smelled good.

"I think they should bomb the whole country and come home," said one of the older men at his table. He was talking loud and so were the men with him. "Bunch of yellow niggers is all they are, ought to bomb the whole damn country into sticks and mud holes, is what I think."

"We just fought them yellow savages, didn't we? God-damn Japs," said one of the other men. He was a fat little guy with a face like a jack-o-lantern.

"Well, it's been a while since then," said the third man at the table. He wore glasses and had on a business suit. The other two were wearing khaki shirts and pants and work boots, and had their hats hanging on the tops of their chairs. The suited man had his hat in a chair beside him. It was a very nice fedora.

"They're still Japs," said the man who had been talking the most. "I say the only good Jap is a dead Jap."

"Actually, they're Vietnamese," said the man in the suit.

"You can call them Siamese or Vietnamese, Chinese, or whatever, but they're all slopes to me."

"China was on our side during the war," the well-dressed man said.

"I don't give a shit," said the loud man. "I don't give a good goddamn one way or another."

"There are women in here," said the waitress from behind the counter where she was standing and eating potato chips out of a bag. "Watch your language and taking the Lord's name in vain."

"What ladies?" said the loudmouth.

"Me, Charles. Me. I'm a lady."

This revelation appeared to startle the loudmouth.

"Yeah, well, sorry, Louise. I got a bit het up."

"Yes you did," she said.

I glanced at the younger men in the booth. They had been talking when I came in, but now they were merely sitting quietly, eating hamburgers and drinking Co-colas out of the bottle.

Right then, a sharp-dressed black man came out of the kitchen and partway into the café. He looked about thirty, in good shape, with his hair cut close to his head. He was holding open the kitchen door, which was on a spring.

"I don't mean to bother," he said, "but we been waiting a long time."

"You got to go back to your place," Louise said. "You got a place back there. You know that."

"I'm just saying we been waiting a long time, and I don't think the cook has even started ours."

"He may not have. We serve white people first. You don't like it, you go on down the road a piece. You might find something there."

"I was just checking," he said.

"You ought not come through the kitchen like that. You go on back now."

The black man seemed to let his thoughts linger in front of him for a moment, and then he went back into the kitchen letting the swinging door swing shut on its spring.

"Damn niggers," Louise said. "They been listening too much to that Martin Luther Coon."

"It's alright if a woman says damn, but I can't say what I said," the loudmouth said.

"It's my place. I can say what I want, and I can serve who I want, and I'm thinking I might not serve those niggers at all. And I didn't use the Lord's name in vain."

She let her face crease, and then she let it un-crease and came around to my table with more coffee. She poured my cup full.

"You doing okay, Sugar?"

"I am," I said. "You want to feed that man first, I'm in no hurry."

"Niggers wait their turn," she said.

"Isn't it his turn?"

"It's his turn when I say it is," she said. "Don't go feeling sorry for niggers. You do, next thing you know they're up on your porch and trying to get their nose in your house. You can't be good to them, they take advantage."

She went around to the table with the older men and filled their coffee cups. They were talking about something or another, but I had tuned them out by then. I kept thinking about that poor man waiting on his food out back and the waitress and the cook not getting it fixed for him.

While I was waiting, Louise went behind the counter and the black man came back through the swinging doors. He said, "Really, we just need three hamburgers and some chips, some Co-colas. We been waiting near an hour."

"Didn't I tell you not to come through the kitchen?" Louise said. "Colored got the porch out there."

"The screened porch with the holes in the screen that flies come through?" said the black man. I could tell he was starting to lose patience.

"You can't come through the kitchen," Louise said.

"There's a black cook in there, he comes through the kitchen."

"When he goes home, he goes out the back way. I ain't going to ask you again. You go on now. Fact is, you pack that nigger family of yours up and get on down the road."

The black man stood there. He was holding the swinging door. "Let me buy some chips and some Co-colas and we'll go on."

"You'll go on, and without chips or Co-colas," Louise said.

The one called Charles, the loudmouth, got up and came to the edge of the counter where it was open and you could go behind it. He was looking right at the black man. He said, "In my day we tarred and feathered smart niggers."

"Your day is still here," the black man said.

This made the older man turn red.

"Yeah," he said, "it is, and sometimes niggers come to the wrong places and talk the wrong kind of talk."

"I'm talking alright," said the black man.

The other khaki-dressed man at Charles' table stood up and came over to stand by the loudmouth.

The older man in the suit didn't move from the table. He said, "Hey, it's alright. Just go on back and wait. They'll get you those burgers."

"No we won't," Louise said. "Get on down the road, coon."

"Look, we been traveling all night. We been traveling a few days now, all the way from New Jersey. We got family in LaBorde. We just want something to eat."

"You can get it somewhere else," Louise said.

"You heard," said Charles the loudmouth.

"I fought for my country," the black man said. "I was in Korea."

This jumped out of his mouth as if it had been hiding behind his teeth, waiting to pounce.

"I was in Korea too." It was one of the younger men at the other booth. They had been so quiet, I had almost forgotten they were there. "Hell, lady, give the man some chips and some Co-colas."

"I'm not doing that." She reached under the counter and pulled out a sawed-off baseball bat and shook it at the black man.

"I was in Chosin Reservoir, so that bat doesn't scare me," said the black man.

"Give me the bat," said the loudmouth. "I can scare him with it."

The black man didn't move. He stood there holding the door to the kitchen open.

"That's enough," said the younger man, and he got up and went over and reached over the counter and snatched the bat from Louise. He tossed it to his buddy in the booth. His buddy caught it, stood up and leaned against the wall by the booth and held the bat against his leg.

"We're done with this stuff," said the younger man. He pulled half a dozen chips loose from the rack and walked past the old man, went behind the counter, and gave them to the black man at the door. He went over and got four Co-colas out of the Coke box, opened them with the opener in the box, walked over to the black man with them, holding the drinks between the fingers of his two hands.

"You better not do that," said Charles the loudmouth.

"Stop me," said the younger man.

Charles did nothing. He remained where he was and boiled.

The black man put the sodas between his fingers, pressing them in tight against the rims of the drinks. He had the bags of chips pinched between his thumbs and forefingers. Both hands were full of all he was going to get that day in that café.

The younger man said, "You ought to go on now."

"Thank you," said the black man.

"I was at Chosin," said the younger man.

"It was hell," said the black man.

"It was more than hell. Now go on. I've done what I can."

The black man went through the kitchen and disappeared with the door swinging shut behind him.

The young man pulled out his wallet and put some bills on the counter, went around it and back to where he had been eating.

"You ought to go on," Louise said. "We don't know you two, and you ought to go on."

"You heard the lady," Charles said.

"Now she's a lady," the other young man said. It was the first time he had spoken.

Their hamburgers were only partially eaten. The young

man who had given the black man the food put some bills on the table and he and his buddy started for the door.

"Nigger lover," said the loudmouth.

"It's alright," said the man in the suit. "You boys are alright. But go on now."

"They ain't alright," said the other man in khakis. "Nigger lovers. Not a damn thing worse. I hate them more than the niggers. Nigger is what he is, but you boys are what you are by choice. One's scum by birth, but you two are the way you want to be."

The young man with the bat dropped it on the floor and he and his companion went out together. There was a window at my booth. I looked out of it. I watched them drive away in a shiny brown Buick.

Louise went to the phone on the wall and dialed someone and spoke soft and I didn't hear it. I could tell she was mad though.

"Tell them they probably took the main road," said Charles. "I doubt that coon is smart enough to keep out of sight, and them other two, they don't figure how bad they've stepped in it. Goddamn niggers. Goddamn nigger lovers."

"Don't call anyone, Louise," the older man in the suit said. "Don't do that. It's not worth it for some chips and Co-colas. That fellow paid you."

"You're sounding like a nigger lover yourself," Charles said. "Don't come around here no more."

"You don't own this café," the man in the suit said.

"But I do," Louise said. "Don't come around anymore. Eat somewhere else. I can't abide a nigger lover."

The older man in the suit got up and opened his wallet and put bills on the table. He was trembling. He put on his hat and went out.

I put money on the table for what I would have eaten, and went on out behind him. I watched the man in the suit walk toward his car. I walked over to him.

"Who would they call?" I said.

"It's best not to know," he said. "It's even best not to think about it."

He got in his car and slammed the door and drove off.

I got in mine and did the same. I tooled on toward Tyler, but after about twenty minutes I turned around and headed home. The air had gone out of my adventure.

I stopped for gas when I came back through No Enterprise, and when I got on down the road, I passed the car the two young men had been in. Their brown Buick was partially off the road and both the front doors were open, but I didn't see them anywhere.

10.
APOLLO RED

"Alright, let me ask this," Leonard said. "Would your father have stood up for that black man in the café?"

"Probably not," I said. "He may have been too much of his time. I hate to say that, but that might be the truth."

"I don't know," Leonard said. "He seems to me to have been a pretty straight shooter."

"In most ways I think he was, but when it came to race, I can't say completely. I mean, yeah, he had his moments. He used to do a lot of things to help black people. I think when it was just him and them, he could be kind and generous. I think the whole thing with whites looking on, well, maybe he could go the other way."

"He was brave, though, and that often says something about a man."

"Bad people can be brave, Leonard. Not that I think he was bad. But, hey, he was brave."

"I know the stories," Leonard said.

"Tell me one, Daddy," Chance said.

I looked at Brett. She was holding her face up with a hand under her chin and an elbow on the table. She had heard all these stories.

"Okay," I said. "There's the one about a guy I call Apollo Red."

"Oh, I love this one," Leonard said.

"Even I feel a bit more alert," Brett said. "I like this one too. And just for the record, I know more stories than I'm going to let you tell about your dad tonight, but I want to put my two cents in and say he has always sounded like a hell of a man to me."

"I guess he was," I said. "He was my hero, flaws and all."

"Tell the story, Daddy."

Summer this happened, I must have been about seventeen, give or take a few months. I was down at the garage with my dad. He was washing tools in gasoline, cleaning them up, getting ready for me and him to drive to the café and get some lunch, though in that day and time we called the noon meal dinner, and the later meal supper. Yankees had lunch. We had dinner.

Dad was always greasy because he always worked. He cleaned up when he was home, but he was the kind of guy that could put on freshly cleaned and ironed khakis, and within an hour at the garage, look as if he had been living inside an oil drum. He worked hard and was good at it. He could fix any kind of car and make it hum. Odd thing was, we always drove junk. I guess it's like the barber who needs a haircut, the dentist who needs his teeth cleaned, the carpenter whose porch is sagging. Dad spent his time working on other people's cars, trying to put food on the table and a roof over our heads.

When he was eight his mother died, and his fondest memory of her was that once for Christmas she had given him an orange and a peppermint stick. He talked about it like it had happened yesterday, like the gift was as important as a new car. For him it was.

His father was a mean-spirited jackass that made Dad work in the cotton fields when he was eight. At that time and place this was acceptable behavior. Once, on the way to the fields, Dad fell off the pinto pony he rode and busted his ear drum. He rode the horse back home, hanging on its back, limp as a blanket.

His father took a horse whip to him, sent him back to work with blood running out of his ear. You'd think with an upbringing like that Dad would have passed it down the line, but he didn't. I never got one whipping, spanking, whatever you want to call it. And I'll tell you, I'm not altogether opposed to a slap on the ass over doing something that is going to get you killed, but that's a far cry from a beating. I never got either from him, though my mother once took a flyswatter to me for something I well deserved. It embarrassed me more than it hurt me.

For a poor kid I was what they called spoiled in those days, and what my mother called loved. Spoiled was going to work at fifteen instead of eight. At the time this happened I was working a night shift at Imperial Aluminum and going to school during the day, but this was the summer, so I was free until three thirty. I got off at midnight. If there were child labor laws against that, neither the boys I worked with or the aluminum chair company we worked for was aware of it.

So there I was, waiting on Dad to clean up a bit, and this guy comes driving up in this shiny gold Cadillac with a golden swan ornament on the hood, kind that was made mostly of plastic. When you turned on the lights the swan lit up. Coming down the road at night you saw the headlights, and dead center of the hood, a golden swan floating across the night, seemingly pulling the car along with stiff-winged elegance. During the day it was just a gold plastic bird with a wire and a bulb inside of it.

The Caddy drove up as we were about to leave, and this raw-boned, redheaded guy with his short shirt sleeves rolled up to display his sizable biceps, got out. His hair was well oiled and slicked back on the sides and he had a bit of a duck tail in the back. He looked as if he were wearing a copper helmet.

He got out and stuck a cigarette in his mouth, walked about halfway up to the wide open garage doors, paused, lit his smoke carefully with a gold lighter, doing it for dramatic effect, like he was posing for a photo, and then he snapped the lighter closed with a metallic clap, stuffed it in his tight pants pocket, and strutted into the garage, his black boots with red explosions on the toe flashing before him. The toes on those things were so long and pointed he could have kicked a cockroach to death in a corner.

The man kind of glowed. It was as if a white trash Apollo had descended from heaven in his golden chariot, down from the sun to get his oil checked, have a chicken-fried steak with white gravy, and screw a mortal before ascending back to the heavens. In my mind I nicknamed him Apollo Red.

There was a lemon-colored Buick parked inside the garage, and it was the car my father had been working on that morning. Dad was drying his hands on a shop rag when this guy swaggered in, leaned a large hand on the Buick, said, "This car fixed yet?"

Dad studied Apollo Red the way a snake studies a frog.

"Yep," Dad said.

"My girlfriend's got to have it."

"Alright," Dad said. And he told the guy what the charge was.

"She'll have to owe you," said Apollo Red.

"Owes me for the last time I fixed it."

"You didn't fix it good enough."

"That was the transmission, this here was a leak in the carburetor. I rebuilt it so she don't have to buy a new one. I saved her about thirty dollars."

"Did, did you?"

Dad just looked at him.

The fellow strayed an eyeball my way. "That your boy?"

"Yeah," Dad said.

"Needs a haircut."

"Yeah, he does."

"I'd hold him down and trim it with a pocket knife."

I had heard this shit a million times, and sometimes it seemed a million times a day. Lot of the boys then had long hair. The girls liked it and so did I. I thought this hair remark was an odd statement coming from a man that wore his hair the way he did. Probably as long as mine, but tamed with hair oil and spray and a lot of mirror examination and a fine-toothed comb. I started to say something smart, but somehow I didn't want to get into Dad's bubble. And something about that guy made me cautious, like knowing to avoid a dark alley at night in a strange city.

"He might need it, but it won't be you cutting it, or two more just like you," Daddy said.

That caused Apollo Red to purse his lips and knit his brows. His gray eyes became slits. Apollo Red thought a moment, almost loud enough to hear his thoughts running about in his head like mice on gravel, and then he turned his attention back to Dad.

"Girlfriend needs the car. She sent me to get it. She can't pay you nothing right now, but she's good for it, and I'm going to take it."

"Naw, she ain't taking it, and neither are you," Dad said. "Shouldn't have worked on it, knowing she don't pay her bills."

"Is that right?"

"Know she works at the beauty parlor and has a long walk to work without a car. Wanted to help her out, but I need at least half what she owes me for the last job. You got that, you can take it, though how you're going to drive two cars is a puzzle."

"I'll pull it out, park it in the lot, bring her to get it when she gets off work. She needs it tonight."

"Tell her to get the money," Dad said, and he was through talking. He walked by Red toward the garage doors. The doors were two wide metal sections you pulled closed and linked with a chain that ran through a hole in the doors, then you padlocked them together. Dad was about to pull the doors when Red said, "Wait a minute, old man."

Now at this time, Dad was pushing sixty, and that was back when sixty was old. He had gained a lot of weight and was tired looking, but back in his younger days he had been a boxer and a carnival wrestler. He had a kind of strength, especially when he was younger, that was almost startling. It wasn't built-up gym stuff, it was working-man muscle, compacted and stretched and flexed by hard work from the time he was a child. He didn't look like much, but neither does a stick of dynamite.

That said, this guy was young and well formed, and he moved like a cat. Just looking at him I knew he had done bad things and wanted to do more. I could feel a crackle in the air when he talked. It's that strange feeling you get when things aren't right, a sensation of something mean and nasty on the other side of some kind of dimensional barrier, waiting to get through a slit in time and space, enter into one of us humans and ignite our most evil traits, send us flailing with fist, snapping with teeth, slashing with knives, slinging clubs, and tossing rocks.

Apollo Red, obviously annoyed, came outside and put his butt to the fender of his car, said, "You ain't going nowhere till you give me that car."

"Going to get something to eat," Dad said.

Apollo Red reached down and took hold of his belt with both hands and hitched it up, like maybe he was making room for a set of testicles the size of bowling balls, and said, "You ain't going nowhere, Greasy, less'n you give me that car."

"Soon as I lock these doors you can watch me and my boy and my greasy clothes drive away, 'cause I'm done talking to you."

This was like tossing gasoline on a fire for Apollo Red. "Tell you what, old man, I'll sort your shit out right now, that's what I'll do."

Dad looked at him. I had seen that gaze before, and let me tell you, you had to be a fucking idiot not to know there was something feral behind those near-black eyes, and that this was a man who had seen the devil and kicked his ass. But the devil had taken his beating twenty years earlier, not of recent from an overweight, old man pushing sixty.

Apollo Red bounced himself off of the car fender, cocked his hand back as he came forward, and I thought, well, I'm stepping in. Dad's getting old, and I better help.

But even though I was no slouch when it came to fighting, I was afraid. Apollo Red wasn't merely a smart-ass kid that wanted to tussle a bit. He was a bad man and you could sense it.

All of these thoughts came quickly, of course, and as I prepared to jump into the fray, Dad lunged forward. He was standing still one moment, and in the next he was covering ground like a bullet.

And then it came. It was an impossibly fast and short uppercut, but it was still a punch from hell. Before Apollo Red's punch could reach him, the upper cut rose, almost touching Red's chest as it tracked toward his chin. To this day I imagine flames coming off of it, Dad was moving so fast. His shot hit while Apollo Red was still bringing his punch around. Dad's flat fat fist caught Apollo Red solid under the chin, and it's the only time in my life I have actually seen someone lifted that high off the ground from a punch. That loudmouth was launched like a space rocket, and the only thing missing was a monkey on board and radio contact with NASA.

The blow made a sickening sound, and that upper cut lifted him onto the fender of his car. He rolled then, caught his shirt in the flying bird hood ornament; tore it half off, and rolled onto the concrete drive. One leg started kicking, like maybe he was trying to stomp a bug in a ditch, and then Apollo Red's head cocked back and he let out with a wheeze similar to steam hissing from a teapot. His eyes rolled up in his head like cherries in a slot machine. I almost expected him to spit coins.

And then he was still.

Corpse still.

I wouldn't have been surprised if vultures were already passing the word.

I went over, leaned down, and looked. Apollo Red's lips were blue. He may have been the sun god where he came from, but the god of lightning and thunder had just knocked the sunlight out of his ass.

I said, "Dad, I think you killed him."

Dad always carried a stub of a cigar in his shirt pocket, and as he walked over he pinched it from his pocket and poked it in his mouth. He scratched around in his pants pockets for a box of matches. When he found them, he took a match out slowly, struck it on the strike-strip on the side of the box, held the flame to that foul-smelling cigar. He shook the match and threw it down. He looked down at Red, turned his head from side to side like a curious dog, said, "Nah. He'll come around."

I wasn't so sure.

"You hit him hard, Daddy."

"Man's punch is the last thing to go."

I guess Dad might actually have been a little concerned, because we didn't go to dinner. He stood near the guy's car for a bit, then went inside and picked up a comic book. He couldn't actually read, but he was learning a bit with Western comics. He liked *Billy the Kid*. I helped him with the words.

"Go get us some hamburgers, Baby Man," he said.

I had anything but dinner on my mind, but in a kind

of daze I drove to the café and got hamburgers, fries, couple of Cokes, and drove back.

This took about thirty minutes or so. Dad was still attempting to read his comic, moving his lips over the words he was learning. Apollo Red still hadn't moved. It had grown really hot.

Dad ate his hamburger and fries, then went back to work on a car at the rear of the garage, his head under the hood, whistling like one of the dwarves from Snow White. Apollo Red, lying on the summer-hot concrete, still had not wiggled a muscle.

I tried to eat, but couldn't. I stood and looked at Red. About an hour after he had taken a ride on the rocket from hell, he twitched.

Like the Frankenstein monster testing his nerves and muscles, starting to recognize shapes and shadows, he writhed against the concrete. His jaw on one side had swollen to about the size of an eggplant and his chin had blackened like a two-day beard. The flesh around the eye on the side of the swelling had gone black as well. There was blood at the corners of his mouth.

Apollo Red stirred a little more. He rolled to one side with no more trouble than a beached whale. He lay there for a while pulling in ultra-violet rays. Birds flew over and dropped their shadows on him. Apollo Red finally got a knee under him, but his head hung low, as if heavy. The position he was in, it looked as if he were about to attempt an impromptu headstand. A tooth fell out of his mouth. He laid back down for a while.

I looked at Dad. He was still doping out the comic book.

Another fifteen or twenty minutes passed, and then Apollo Red moved again. He went through all the formations he had managed before, but this time, when it came to the knee position, he pushed up to his feet, wobbled a bit, and then forgetting he had come by car, started slowly zig-zagging away, as if practicing evasive maneuvers against a slow-moving, heat-seeking missile.

He staggered across the street, over the dead grass next to the oil well bit shop, fell down, got up with excruciating slowness, continued to zig-zag until he stumbled out of sight behind a high stack of tires at the rear of a filling station.

I finally ate my hamburger. Dad went back to work. I sat around for another hour. I had planned to eat dinner with Dad, go home and go to work, but I decided the hell with it. I was too shook up. I walked across to the bit shop, borrowed their phone, called my boss, said I would be in late, if at all.

There was only one old man there that day, and he grinned what teeth he had at me. "I seen him hit that sucker," he said, and pointed to a window in the side of the aluminum building to show me the exact spot where he had stood. "Damn. Bud's still got the punch, ain't he?"

"Yes, sir," I said. "Appears he does."

By the time I crossed back to the garage, a police car pulled up alongside Apollo Red's golden chariot. There with a young policeman on the passenger side, an older hand I recognized behind the wheel. He had once pulled me in for throwing water balloons. I nodded at him, like an experienced criminal acknowledging a foe.

The one on the passenger side, the younger one, got out as Dad came wandering out of the shop. Dad leaned against the hood of Red's car, which bore part of Red's shirt on the broken hood ornament like some sort of surrender flag. I came over and stood by Dad.

The young cop said, "Mr. Collins. There's been a complaint that you hit a man here."

"Hard as I could," Dad said.

"He has a broken jaw and is at the hospital and is a little confused."

"He was confused when he got here," Dad said.

The young cop nodded. "Well, sir, why'd you do it?"

"Threatened me."

"How?"

"Tried to hit me?"

"Did he?"

"Too slow."

The young cop computed this, said, "Sir, you have to come with us downtown. There's been a complaint. His girlfriend filed it."

"I don't think so," Dad said.

"You don't think what?" said the young cop.

"I don't think I'm coming."

The older cop behind the steering wheel leaned across the seat, and said through the open door, "Bud, you really got to come."

Dad turned his head in that curious dog way. "That you, Clyde?"

"Yes, sir."

"You know me," Dad said.

"Yes, sir," Clyde said.

"You know I'm not coming."

Clyde cleared his throat. "We're supposed to bring you in."

"Folks make plans."

The young cop, feeling the drift of things, stepped back and put his hand on his gun.

Dad reached out and gently pushed me away from him. The older cop said, "Dean. Get back in the car."

Dean stood there with his hand on the butt of his revolver. He was sweating. The cop cap on his head seemed too big all of a sudden. I noted that the distance between him and Dad was not a lot different from the distance between Dad and Apollo Red when he had leaped forward and hit him.

"Dean," Clyde said. "Get back in the car."

After a long moment, Dean uncoiled and moved his hand from the gun.

Dad had not so much as changed his expression.

Dean got back in the car and closed the door.

They drove away and never came back.

Next day, when Dad went back to work, Red's car was gone, and about two weeks later the woman who owned the Buick came in and paid him all she owed, saying only, "How much?"

I was there that day, having dropped by to go to dinner with Dad again. The woman was a nice-looking blonde with a lot of hairspray on her hair; it formed a little blue cloud around her head when the sunlight hit it. I wanted to ask her if Apollo Red knew his own name and still remembered how to drive a car. I knew for sure he wasn't the one who had come for it. Apollo Red had descended, and would not be ascending for quite some time.

"It was the carburetor this time," Dad told her. "You might ought to think on getting some tires, too. These are may-pops."

"Yes, sir," said the lady.

Dad gave her the keys.

As she was slipping behind the wheel of her car, starting it up, Dad said, "Come on back, it gives you any trouble."

11.
COACH WHIP

"But you don't know anything happened to them," Chance said.

"I think I do."

"It did, baby girl," Leonard said. "Those were the times. In East Texas, you were expected to take one side or another, and if you were black you knew your place, and if you were white you were worried about your place. That's how it was. Not that everyone stuck to that, thank goodness. Me and Hap here, we ought to have hated one another, but we didn't, and we bearded the lions in their dens so much, it's amazing we have survived."

"Yeah, some people never learn that things aren't as they appear to be, or they aren't as they should be. I got a lesson in that when I was little. I guess you can call it a true story with a parable attached. My dad was responsible for the latter part."

———————

When I was young, my dad's job played out, so we decided to drive from East Texas to Arizona, where some of our family lived. They said there were jobs there, and Dad needed a job, so away we went.

It was hot on the road in that old, black car of ours, and there wasn't any air-conditioning in it, so we had the windows rolled down to bring in the breeze. I loved it when we drove at night. I would lie on my back and stuff my pillow behind my head and watch the stars through the back window. The air would blow in so that the inside of the car was quite cool. I'd pull a blanket over me and dream that I was in a space ship flying amongst the stars. I had my dog with me, my faithful space hound Blackie, who was small and fuzzy with a heart like a water buffalo. He would snuggle close to me, the wind fluttering his ears, and we would soon be asleep.

I loved that dream, and sometimes now, when I can't sleep, I have the same one. That I have had a great adventure, and that I'm recovering in my little space craft the size of my bed, and I have my battle-ready friend at the controls. Sometimes in my dreams the battle-ready friend is my fine redheaded woman, Brett, and she's dressed like Dale Arden from Flash Gordon, and she is guiding us carefully through the solar system in our swift space/bed machine. Sometimes it is an unknown driver, a comrade in arms. I feel safe and it helps me sleep.

But back then I was just a kid, and I never felt safer than when I was with my parents, especially my father who could bend coins with his hands and crush an apple in his palm, expand his chest and break belts, or bend metal bars, so he was at the controls, sliding our little black space ship through the infinite blackness, sprinkled with stars.

At night we would stop at tourist courts, as they were called then, the forerunners of modern motels, and we would spend the night. Sometimes we didn't have the money, and we slept in the car, but if my dad could find day work, and it was easier in some ways to find it then than now, he would be able to make enough to buy us food and a place to stay for the night and put gas in the car. He also had his shotgun with him, and there were a few times when we stopped along the way and he went out into the woods to hunt squirrels, which after shooting he cleaned quickly and expertly with a pocket knife, then we cooked the meat on a hot plate in tourist court rooms. My dog ate the scraps of our meals.

Once in a town in Arizona we made a wrong turn and ended up in a downtown parade. I don't know what it was for, perhaps a local celebration, but once we were in the parade with floats and other cars and young ladies in truck beds wearing bathing suits and waving at the crowd, we couldn't get out. Every time my dad tried to turn out of the parade there seemed to be a policeman there with a whistle and gestures pointing him back into position. We rode like members of the parade, our windows down, my little dog rearing up and looking out one of them, barking. Somewhere along the line, when no policeman was around and there was a clear exit, Dad broke for it and drove us away from the parade and back on track. I missed the parade. It was a fun thing to have happen.

We drove during the day looking for work, and the sun beat down and the wind blew through the windows. I had no idea we were poor and were sort of doing our own Joad moment on the road. My parents picked vegetables and fruit and cotton on the way, day laborers. Sometimes if the work was good we would stay a few days and build up our cash supply. I helped do some of the work since no one was keeping children from working, but all I remember about that was trying to pick cotton and getting so hot I ended up with heat exhaustion and had to lay out under a tree in the shade for most of the day, sipping water from what we called a jug that had once been an old pickle jar.

When we arrived at our relatives' home, we stayed with them for a few days while my dad found work somewhere. Perhaps it was mechanic work, more likely some kind of farm work as a field hand. I remember him doing both along the way, and after we arrived, he went daily to some job or another, came home at night tired and hungry.

We ended up renting a ramshackle place not far from where the relatives lived. It was a house that had settled down until it touched the ground. The porch itself lay flat against the dirt and the wooden steps in front of it stood higher. We never used those, and finally my dad pried them apart with a crow bar and moved the wood away from the porch. That way all we had to do was step about two inches higher than the ground. There was a chicken coop there, and if we cared for the chickens, it cost us less, so therefore we cared for the chickens. I remember my mother in the dirt yard calling, "Chick, chick, chick, here chick, chick."

This mass of chickens would come darting and clucking out of the open hen house and into the yard, where my mother stood with a pail of dried corn, tossing it to them by the handfuls, as they came pecking at it across the sun-hardened ground.

We ate a lot of pinto beans and cornbread. On Sunday we went to our better-off relatives for Sunday dinner. Dinner is what folks call lunch these days. We called the late meal supper. At the relatives we had fried chicken and biscuits, and all manner of delights, including homemade apple pie. Everything was home grown and homemade. One night I remember us being so in need of food my mother cooked up some of the hen scratch, as she called it, meaning the thick corn kernels used as chicken feed, and we ate that. I don't remember it tasting too bad. She cooked it the consistency of mush, and that's what she called it as well. Mush. When I was growing up, when we had more money to buy cornmeal, she made me that for breakfast, pouring milk onto it and stirring butter in.

As I said, the place we rented came with a chicken house and chickens, and part of our rent was gathering eggs for the owner, and being allowed to keep some. We were also allowed to eat some of the chickens, and besides the Sunday dinner of fried chicken we had at the relatives' house, once a week we ate one or two of the chickens, ones that weren't good layers, or older roosters who were past their time. New chicks were being born constantly and they grew swiftly. My dad, when he killed chickens, wrung their necks. He would grasp one by the head, sometimes one in each hand, clamp tight, and with a twist and a swinging motion, break their necks. Sometimes he could pop the heads completely off, and other times the necks stretched out long and they looked like short hoses with chicken bodies swinging on them. He would toss the chicken on the ground, and dead, or near death, it would get up and run around. This happened sometimes when you chopped a chicken's head off, hence the phrase run around like a chicken with its head cut off. It was terrifying to see either a headless chicken, or a neck wrung chicken with its dangling neck and head, running about until it finally fell over.

Once me and my dog Blackie went out to collect eggs in the hen house, and there was a chicken snake in it. We surprised one another. I lifted up a hen's ass to grab an egg for Mom to cook for my breakfast, and found the snake curled beneath the hen. Me and the snake were traumatized, and when the chicken realized that somehow from below the snake had found its way into her nest and was under her ass, she too was traumatized. She leaped off her perch and went batting her wings around the chicken house and squawking wildly, stirring up all the other chickens, causing a cacophony of squawks. The snake lay still in the nest, its body swollen with eggs. Sulfur and cayenne pepper mixtures, moth balls, and other things of that sort were placed around the outside of the hen house, as they were supposed to discourage snakes, but the chicken snake had ignored them. To it, a keep out sign would have been about as efficient.

I know this. I was through with that hen house, never went back into one until I was in my early teens. And even then, I was nervous. Snakes are something country people grow up with, and fear of them is hard-wired into our brain, and more often than not, for no real reason.

I remember seeing a sidewinder moving along a hot, red sand path near where we were staying back then, slipping along in that peculiar S fashion they have. The manner of locomotion itself terrified me. Just didn't seem right. Snakes back home could be scary, and we had rattlers too, and the sidewinder is a rattler, but the ones back home didn't move like that. Not only could they scare you and bite you, they moved creepy.

Not far from where we were was an old quarry. I'm not sure what they had mined there, but it was played out by this time. It was a big place and it was full of water. I wasn't supposed to go anywhere near it, but its mystery drew me to it as simply and profoundly as the proverbial moth to a flame. I would sneak off from time to time and go there. I would stand on the edge of it and stare at the still water. My older cousins would come over and they would go swimming in it, but I wouldn't. It was too deep. And besides, I couldn't swim. My father had lost a friend in the Sabine River once, when he was a kid. He and his buddy got pulled into a whirlpool. My dad was able to swim out, as he was strong even as a child, but his friend was pulled into the suck hole and drowned. He never forgot it, of course, and that story stuck with me, and my mother was afraid of water, electricity, gas, just about everything, including snakes, so you can bet I had my fears, especially back then. I've made a point over the years to either get rid of all of them, or to find a way to confront them. One of those fears was that great quarry full of water. Still, I was drawn to it, to stand near the edge of it and look out at the water and wonder at the depths of it; the fear of falling into it had a hypnotic draw.

I hated being there in that Arizona heat, out there in a place that made me feel blue, the air so dry it made my skin itch. I don't like places where there isn't greenery, and I don't enjoy seeing for long distances. Empty expanses make me sad. East Texas had lots of tall trees and water, creeks and ponds, and man-made lakes. I don't know how much of that I understood back then, but I knew this wasn't where I had been living, and I didn't care for it.

It was still bright and hot and the sun was just beginning to dip. I stood on the edge of the quarry and watched the water in it turning purple with shadow. Blackie wasn't with me. For some reason he had stayed back at the house. The heat maybe. Or maybe I had ditched him on purpose. It was hard to sneak off and go some place I wasn't supposed to be because he would actually run back to the house barking, and my mother, who would figure out I was where I wasn't supposed to be, would come after me. I loved my dog, but he was a snitch.

Kids, including my two cousins, swam in the quarry. There was a path where the rocks had tumbled down and some of the older kids and my cousins would skinny dip. I didn't know any of them, and it made me nervous to see them going down there, stripping off their clothes, boys and girls, and I kept thinking they might want to pull my pants down and throw me in. I was very modest in those days, and still am when it gets right down to it, and I had a fear not only of that, but that they would throw me into the water and make me swim, which I couldn't. I don't know why I felt that way, but I did. Actually, I don't think they even noticed me. I remember watching the kids swim for a while, amazed at their white skin in the darkening water.

Eventually they climbed out, dressed, and went home, and I watched them go along the far side of the quarry, then I started home. The sun dipped even more and the sky bled over the earth and gathered up in the handful of scrub trees along the way home. I walked swiftly, wanting to be home before the sun went down and my mother started calling for me. I had already pushed my time, and my guess was she thought I was still in the yard playing.

The path was red and sun-bleak. There were some mountains in the distance, and the mountains held the shadows to them like possessions, and the darkness in their crags and crannies gave me a feeling of unease that is impossible to explain.

I was really missing those East Texas trees and all the creeks and ponds and sandy trails. When the sun went down in East Texas the woods and the greenery turned emerald, and the shadows between the trees were mysterious and lovely. This place turned red and sad and the shadows began to look like oil stains.

I walked along the hardened dirt road with red sand on either side, and even at the dying of the day, it made everything hot. It was so hot I could feel it through my tennis shoes. I still remember that. I remember that in East Texas as well, but there always seemed there was shade to be had, and when it was night the ground cooled quickly. There is much that is embraced and loved about dry heat compared to humidity, but when I sweat I know I'm hot, and I don't keep moving about and end up falling out. The East Texas sweat cools me when I find shade and be still, but in that dry heat of Arizona I think I'm fine until I'm not.

Bake or fry, when you get right down to it, doesn't matter, I suppose.

In time I came to where there was dead grass growing on either side of the trail. The grass was the color of crackers and there was no wind to move it, but I saw that in one spot it was moving, rustling ever so gently. I stopped and looked. I didn't see anything at first. The grass stopped swaying. A moment later it began to move again, and a dark head rose up from the grass.

The head swayed first to one side and then the other, and there was a little forked tongue that came out of its mouth, blue-looking, and it snapped at the red-shaded air, and then the head went down and the grass began to move again. It was coming right for me.

I came unstuck and started running, sure I would get away from the snake quickly, but when I looked back I saw it coming along the trail now, moving briskly, squirming its way after me, all three or four feet of it, its head lifted like a periscope as it moved speedily along.

I ran faster. Glancing back, I saw that it was still coming, and it was closing on me, and I didn't have one doubt in the world that it was pursuing me and perhaps wanted to bite me in the ass on general principles. When I saw the rent house was in sight, I began to yell for my mother.

I was a short ways from the house when my mother came out on the porch and saw me running. I don't think she saw the snake right away, but as I came up on the porch she did. Grabbing at me, she pulled me inside and shut the door.

My dog had stirred by now, though he wasn't supposed to be inside the house, as in those days that was thought of as bad housekeeping. But, my parents loved that dog as much as I did, and that's where he stayed. We looked out one of the porch windows, me, Mom, and Blackie. That snake was on the porch, and it raised its head and looked in the window at us, swaying from side to side. I jumped back and I think I started screaming, because I had no doubt in my mind that it was me it wanted. Blackie, due to my screaming, began to run around me in circles, barking.

My mother said, "You stay here," and went out the back door. After a moment she appeared on the front porch with a hoe in her hand. The hoe flashed out, missed the snake, and the snake turned away from the window and went along the porch away from my mother, but she chased after it. I positioned myself to see out the window, and the last thing I saw of the snake was its tail whipping off the porch and out of sight, and then my mother chasing after it, the hoe raised above her head like a cartoon character.

I don't know how long my mom was gone, but finally I saw her through the window. She came up on the porch and put the hoe against the wall, and came inside. She was always dramatic, and she leaned against the door frame as if she had just been in a great battle that she had only marginally survived.

"I killed it," she said. "I chopped its head off."

Late afternoon, suppertime, my father came home.

Mother related our snake adventure, and how she had killed it, and protected us, because that snake wanted in, and when she was through telling her story that snake could have been an army of snakes.

My dad went outside to look at the snake. I went out with him. Even though it was dead, I wouldn't get near it. I could see that its head had been chopped off, but I had heard even a headless snake didn't die until sundown. I had heard a lot of mythical stories about snakes, including the one about the hoop snake which grabbed its tail in its mouth and rolled down hill like a tire. There was also the snake that was said to slip under cows, attaching itself to one of their udders, and sucking out the milk, which was a reason some farmers said a milk cow went dry. I had known plenty of grown-ups to tell those stories for the truth, as absurd as they were.

My dad looked at the snake, then looked at me.

"Come here, son," he said.

I eased closer, but still a goodly distance away from the dead snake.

He said, "See the way it looks. It don't have a triangle head. It ain't poisonous. It's not a copperhead, rattler, or water moccasin, and it sure ain't no coral snake. It gets cornered, it'll beat its tail so it sounds like a rattlesnake, but it's not even close. It's a coach whip. They'll chase you sometimes, but they ain't gonna hurt you. Had you stopped running, it would have stopped, and had you ran toward it, it would have run in the other direction. Get it cornered, it'll bite, but ain't no poison in it, but you get anything cornered, it'll fight back. Thing is, boy, not everything that looks scary is. You got to know something well enough before you decide on it as being one way or another."

I wasn't convinced, but that was all he had to say. He went inside, and I went inside after him. For a few days when I woke up at night and turned toward the bedroom window, I imagined I saw that snake rising up in the moonlight to look in at me. I didn't care if all it wanted was to play chase. I didn't care that it didn't have a triangular head or that it wasn't poison. The idea of it terrified me.

Much to my pleasure, we didn't stay in Arizona long. None of us liked it and the jobs weren't that good. We drove up into Colorado, and my dad found work there, and then we drove back through New Mexico and West Texas, Central Texas, Dad and Mom finding field work along the way, and then finally we were back in East Texas, back in Marvel Creek where I had been born, and the air seemed right and the sky seemed right and the woods were dark and green and it rained a lot. I was home.

Some years later, when I was a teenager, I was out walking in the woods behind our house, down near the creek, and I saw the grass rustle. My skin crawled. I stopped and looked. I started walking away, fast, and whatever it was started moving toward me through the grass, and pretty soon I was overcome with what I had felt as a child. I started running like a gazelle.

At some point I remembered what Dad had said, and I found the courage to stop and turn and run back toward where the grass was moving, expecting the snake to run. It didn't. The grass was still moving, and finally the grass parted, and the snake squirmed onto the sandy trail. It wasn't a coach whip. It was a short, stubby water moccasin, one of the poisonous snakes that are partial to East Texas. I have had many people tell me since they won't do that, chase you, I mean, but that one did; it not having read the recent literature. I think a snake in the wild is not a snake in captivity. Maybe snakes make decisions that are not only based on instinct. Maybe now and then they just like messing with you, because that one was certainly chasing me, and I was running as fast as I could go, and it was making easy time toward me.

I glanced back again, and all of a sudden the snake slithered off the trail and into the grass on the other side, and away through it.

That snake had fooled me. I got a lesson out of it, though I don't think I really understood it until years later. Sometimes you can think something is going to hurt you and it isn't, but you can also think something isn't, and it will. I don't know the snake was dead set on catching up with me, because if it had wanted to, it would have. Maybe it was merely waiting to reach its turnoff. But still, I had convinced myself this time that I was being silly and the snake wasn't poisonous, was a coach whip, but it wasn't. Had I chased into the grass after it, and stepped on it, it might have bitten me.

That may have been what Dad was trying to tell me. It's the same way with people. You might see them coming from a long distance off, but you don't know what kind of snake they are just by sight, and they don't have a triangular head to judge by.

12.
THE BOTTOM OF THE WORLD

"My father damn sure had his moments, like telling me about that snake, but telling me something else in the process, teaching me a lesson. He could be contradictory, and there's no doubt he was racist. He hated blacks as a race but tended to like them as individuals. I think he couldn't quite understand if a black person could do better than him, because that didn't seem right. He had grown up with nothing, and the idea that there were people making fantastic amounts of money always seemed like a lie to him, or if it was true, he felt it was undeserved. I guess you grow up with nothing, ignorant and uneducated, it's hard to wrap your head around that. It didn't seem right to him that anybody ought to make the kind of money they did in sports, for example. Especially black athletes. On the other hand, he had a way of telling me things that mattered through moments like the one with that snake. Now and again he did it through stories."

"I think I'd have liked your dad, me being black or not," Leonard said.

"I don't think he would have liked you," I said. "But, you two are actually a lot alike. In the tough and straight-forward department."

"I'm charming," Leonard said. "He'd have come around."

"You're not only black, but gay, so, I don't know."

"What kind of stories did he tell you?" Chance asked.

"All kinds. Sometimes things that happened to him. Sometimes even a ghost story now and again."

"Oh, I like scary stories," Chance said. "Can you tell me one of his ghost stories?" I glanced at Brett.

Brett smiled. "She's a grown woman, Hap. She can take a ghost story. If not, she and Buffy can cuddle on the couch afterwards."

"See," Chance said, "I'm all grown up." She smiled her dazzling smile. She did that, it was near impossible to deny her anything.

"Alright," I said.

The little electric heater buzzed like a bee and its grillwork glowed cherry red. Hap Collins, ten years old, sat on the floor with his arms clutching his knees, which he had pulled up close to his chest to create warmth. The house was dark except for the heater light. Outside, rain pecked at the glass and the wind howled as if it were a wolf in misery.

There was a scratching sound, and Hap nearly jumped to his feet. But then he remembered what it was. It was the branch of a magnolia tree near the window and when the wind blew hard, the branch moved and touched the window, making that sound. It reminded him of a cat scratching in gravel. Still, familiar as it had become in the last couple of months, it never failed to startle him.

Hap was glad he had his own bedroom though. He had hoped for one. They had been living in tourist courts for the last few months, traveling across Arizona and West Texas so his parents could work the fields and orchards. They picked fruit, cotton, dug potatoes, whatever job was available, until they ended up back in East Texas. But now his dad had a job at a propane company as a trouble shooter, a mechanic. That's what his dad loved doing, fixing cars, and he was good at it. Hap would be in a new school in a few days, in January after the Christmas holidays, and it would be 1960. He thought, new year, new house, and he liked both changes. It was nice to have a house of their own, even if it was cold and a little scary and he was behind in school for having been out for a while until they got settled. Another thing was he didn't know any of the kids in the neighborhood. Yet, it was all exciting to think about.

The bedroom door cracked, and a large man-shaped shadow fell through it, the hall light at its back.

"Son?" said the shadow. "You okay?"

"Yeah," Hap said. "Daddy, would you tell me a story?"

"A story? Do you know what time it is?"

"No."

"It's . . . Well, it's late."

"You're up, Daddy."

"Came to check on you."

The shadow came into the room wearing boxer shorts and sat down on the floor near him. The heater spread its light on the shadow, and the shape was a shadow no longer. The light glowed on a stocky man with thinning hair with forearms as big as baseball bats. His chest was thick. His hands were thick and the fingers were short and blunt at the tips. One time his dad had torn a phone book in half to win a bet with his brother-in-law. It wasn't a very big phone book, actually, but the brother-in-law couldn't do it. He couldn't lift up the back of a car long enough to pull a flat tire off the rim either, but Hap knew his dad could. He'd seen him do it. He didn't know it was a big thing until he started hearing about it from others who had seen it with him. When they spoke of his dad's physical strength they spoke of it in awe.

"Can you tell me a story? A scary one?"

"You look like you might be a little scared now, let alone me tell you some kind of story like that. You ain't got a thing to worry on, Baby Man. The wind is just the wind and the rain is just the rain, and that ole tree is just a tree. In the summer you'll be able to play under it, though that magnolia tree will bring in the bees. You got to watch for them bees."

Hap remembered his mom saying the only thing in the world his dad was afraid of were wasps and bees. A sting from one of them could lay him low for days. He could take a punch thrown by a man twice his size and give him one back three times harder, and he might even be able to outwrestle an alligator and feed it to a bear and make him like it, but a bee or wasp made him nervous.

"I like scary stories," Hap said.

"Yeah. I know. I seen all them comic books you read."

"Tell me, please?"

"Alright. Well, you know we live not far from the river bottoms. All that rich bottom land and the river rolling down through them trees, them trees thick, and it all dark down there. There's all kinds of stories go with it. But they're just stories. And you want to stay away from that river. I was a boy, about your age, my friend Ronnie, me and him went swimming down there, and a whirlpool got him. It almost got me."

"Really?"

"Yeah. We lived not far from where we are now. Whirlpool sucked Ronnie right under, and I was near pulled in too, but I was a stronger swimmer, and I come out of it, but that water felt like it was pulling at my legs, trying to drag me under with him. I guess I kicked free of the thing down there."

"What kind of thing?"

"They say there was this woman lived down there on the banks of the Sabine, and she was young and pretty, and she had a lot of men wanted to marry her. But she

197

didn't never let that happen. She was looking for the right one, and wasn't none of them suited her, you see.

"Well now, one day she sees a man near her cabin, and he's fishing with a cane pole, waiting patiently for a fish, sitting under an old willow tree. Now the woman, near girl really, she looks out and sees this man, and she thinks he's the best-looking fellow she's ever seen, including some in the Sears and Roebuck catalogue."

"Like them that just got on underwear and stuff?"

"Like any of them. So she looks out and sees him, and she thinks, he's the man I want, and she is bold, and goes down there to meet him. He likes her too, right away, and they become . . . friends. Close friends. So the days go by, and finally this young man decides that another young woman he saw in town might be better suited to him, 'cause not only is she pretty, but she has some money too. But the thing is, the river woman, she don't want to let him go, 'cause they done gone and got married, and she ain't gonna let him get shed of her. Arguing goes on for a while, but he can't get her to agree to a divorce, and all this sets heavy on him.

"Then one summer night he does a foolish thing. Wearing nothing but his undershorts, he takes her down to the river, drags her down there by her hair, and her wearing nothing but a flimsy old night gown. He throws her in and goes in after her, pushes her out to the middle of the river. It's not fast moving there, but it's deep, and though she's done spent most of her life on that river all by herself, she never has learned to swim good, and it don't help this fellow is holding her by the hair, and is pushing her under, and it don't take long before she's drowned.

"Now he's got a problem. He's done gone and killed her and now he's got a body. He leaves her in the river she's just gonna float, and though he could say she drowned out there swimming, or slipped on the bank fishing and ended up in the water, he knows ain't no one going to believe that, because she never did swim, and everyone knew she was right afraid of water, and everyone knew too she didn't like to do no fishing, and in fact, she didn't like to eat fish.

"This fellow, he figures thing for him to do is get an old tow sack and put it over her head, and in another sack put an old anvil, tie it to her feet, and drop her out there in the middle of the river where it's deep, where there's a hole there so far down some say it ain't got no bottom. He took her out there in a row boat and dumped her over the side in that bottomless hole in the river. He put her in first with that bag over her head, and he was about to toss the anvil and the chain it was linked up to over the side, when the woman started moving in the water. She wasn't dead. He thought she was dead, but she wasn't.

"He took the boat paddle and went to hitting on her head in that bag. He beat it with everything he had and finally it wasn't moving. Just floating there, her feet was lifted up out of the water on the chain that was fixed onto the anvil in the boat, so she hasn't gone nowhere yet. When he figures he's finally got her settled, he throws that anvil into the water, nearly turning the boat over along with it. Well, that anvil hits the water and it jerks that woman straight down, way down there in that bottomless hole, and this fellow, he's got some relief now, 'cause he figures he's good and quit of her.

"That night he goes back to the house, thinking on how he'll say she run off with another man, and how after a time he'll get a divorce, saying she's run off from him."

"What's a divorce, Daddy?"

"It's a thing some people do when they can't get along, or are just too damn selfish to try and make a thing work. Anyway, this fellow, he's thinking in a while he'll get with that good-looking woman in town that he's been sneaking around and seeing, and with her will come all her money. But back in the house, the wife drowned now, he starts feeling lonely. He starts thinking on her, seeing strands of her hair in her brush on the dresser, a photograph or two around the house with him and her in it. Time he goes to bed, he's upset with himself some, tossing and turning, seeing in his head her tumbling down and down and down in that dark, old, night water, just a twisting around in circles, her hair swaying in the river, her body swirling in that watery hole that ain't got no bottom.

"Finally he goes to sleep, and then he wakes 'cause he hears something. Like someone calling his name, and he knows that voice, or thinks he does, but it don't sound just right. You see, it's got this gurgle about it, like someone is trying to talk with a mouthful of water.

"He thinks, now that can't be her. She's in that river

in that bottomless hole, going down, down, down, that anvil tugging at her toes. But then he hears something that makes his blood grow cold. There's a rattling noise, like the way a plow chain will shake when you're hooking up a mule to plow, and then there's another sound, a dragging sound, like maybe that chain is hooked up to something heavy, and someone has hold of that chain and is dragging that something heavy."

"It's her, ain't it, Daddy?"

"So he gets up and he gets his old shotgun out of the closet, one of them double barrels, and he sits on the edge of his bed, thinking maybe he's dreaming, and he's still lying there under the sheet, and that he didn't hear nothing for real, and didn't get up and get his shotgun. But that sounds just keeps a coming. A little louder now, that chain rattling, that dragging sound, and then . . . It stops. He don't really know where it stops, but he feels like he does. He feels like he knows it's outside the front door, and then there's a calling sudden-like, and it's that same voice with the gurgle in it. It's his wife's voice, like the way it would sound if she was full of water and trying to talk. She's calling his name. Ain't nothing else she's saying other than his name, over and over and over.

"He don't move. He just keeps on sitting there on the edge of the bed, shivering now, and it ain't cold a bit, but he feels wet as if he was in that river again. The voice calls and calls, and then it stops. It stops for a long time, but he don't move none, not a bit. And you know what happens next?"

"What?"

"Something starts a knocking at the door. Slow and steady, and then the knocking stops, and there's a scratching, like a cat, but still he don't move. And then that stops, and he hears that sound again, the chain and something heavy as it goes dragging around the house and comes to the window by the bed. He has his back to that window, but he's heard that sound moving around to it, and he knows without looking that someone or some kind of thing is at that window. So slowly he turns and looks. And damn if there ain't a water-fat face pushed up against the window pane, starring in at him.

"He jumps up then, whirls and fires that shotgun, blasting a load through the glass and into that face, but that face don't do nothing but come apart some, and not much. And he knows it's just who he expected it was. It's his wife, and she's done come for him. She gets hold of the window sill and starts climbing through that window, that broken glass all around it not bothering her none. Hell, he's done shot her right in the face with one load from that double barrel, and she's still a coming, and only looking as bad as she looked before, which is bad enough. Though now she's got little buckshot holes all in her face and head and throat. And she's so white. So white. And there's no blood on her, just them holes, black and small as seed ticks. In she comes, the nightgown torn and ragged around her from her rising up from the river and walking through the close brush, and she's got that chain fastened to her foot, and she bends down and takes hold of that chain, and goes to tugging, pulling that anvil toward her, causing it to drag loud on the ground until it comes scraping up the side of the house and bumps over the open window and falls to the floor with a sound like a big tree falling.

"He can't run. He ain't got the legs for it. His knees is knocking together, and he is stuck there like his feet are nailed to the floor. He does open up on her with that other barrel, but he might as well have tried to tickle her ass with a feather, for all the hurt it does her.

"Closer she comes, holding the chain in her hands, dragging that anvil across the floor. And still he's frozen. Step by wet step she comes, that heavy anvil making groove marks in the wood, and about the time he's come unstuck and is going to run, she moves faster than she ought to be able to, than anyone ought to be able to, and she's done let go of the chain and has grabbed him by the neck. She winds fingers in his hair and pulls him as she turns, and now she's dragging him by the hair, through the house, and to the front door, and when she come to it she just kicks it and it flies off its hinges and out into the yard, and still she comes, dragging him by the hair, her foot pulling the chain and what's hooked up to it.

"Out she goes, slow and steady, dragging him over the ground by the hair to the river. And then she goes into it, floating out to the center of the river where there's that deep old hole, the chain coming after her, that anvil swinging down below her, but still she keeps atop the water, doing what she couldn't do in life, swim, or at least float. When she's right in the center, she tugs him up and looks right at him, plants her water-thick lips on his in a sloppy wet kiss, and then she just lets that anvil pull her down. And away they go, whirling faster and faster, down, down, down in that deep dark hole filled with water, and now with them two lost souls.

"You'd think that'd be the end of it, but it ain't. She's still out there in the river, and where she went down, it's not only deep enough to flow somewhere out of China, the water is spinning around and around on the top of the river, the way it did when she and that man of hers was going down, pulled by that chain and anvil. That water ain't never stopped spinning there since, and that old suck hole don't like men at all, or boys. That's why it took Ronnie. That's why it tried to take me, and that's why over the years it's pulled down many a good boy that's tried to swim it. It's even tugged down row boats, tugged them down in that deep, bottomless hole where's she got her a big old bunch of men and boys, just a spinning around and around in that deep, dark, water hole. Which is why you don't never want to go out in that river to swim, 'specially not in that fast, deep water over the hole. 'Cause that Water Witch, which is what she's come to be called, she's waiting."

Hap sat silent a moment.

"That's near here?"

"It is."

"Is she real?"

"It's a story."

"If it was real, could she come back out of that water?"

"I don't think so. Not anymore. She's stuck there now. She got the man done what he did to her, and now she's got that spot that's hers, and hell to the fellow that tries to swim or fish there. But she can't come out no more. She's stuck right there with that husband of hers, Ronnie, and all them others. Now, you need to get in bed."

Hap slipped under the covers. The covers were warm. His dad tucked them in around him.

"I hate I told you that story," his dad said.

"I liked it."

"But you'll have nightmares, and not only is that bad for you, but Mama will know if you do, and that's bad for both of us."

"I like stories, Daddy."

"Good. I can sleep here beside you if you're scared."

"I'm okay."

"Alright, then," his dad said, and eased out of the room, once again becoming a shadow.

The heater hummed. The wind blew. The rain splattered. The house creaked. Hap envisioned that woman, all swollen up from the water, that chain on her foot, that heavy anvil at the end of the chain, and her spinning around and around just beneath the water, ready to grab a foot and pull you under. He found the story scary, but he found it comforting too. His dad had told him a story like he asked, and the kind of story he asked for, and he loved him for it.

Hap closed his eyes.

Around and around that woman spun. Her hair flowing about like spilled ink, waving in the current, dragging fellows deep down into the wet dark with her, all the way to the bottom of the world.

13.
SQUIRREL HUNT

"You know, Leonard, now that I think about it, I believe he would have stood up for that black man. I really do. He was a man of his time, but he was an honorable man, and had a true sense of fair play."

"I don't doubt that. My uncle never got over me being gay, but honestly, I think he and your dad were a lot alike. Had they known each other in a later time, they might have been friends, like us, thick as thieves."

"You're probably right," I said. "Dad, in spite of his background, had a kind of wisdom about him, and a way of imparting it to you."

"What kind of way?" Chance said.

"A backwoods kind of way," I said.

"See," Brett said. "Backwoods. Like your own father. You can take the boy out of the woods and pick the ticks off of him, but you can't take the woods out of the boy . . . Or something like that."

"It's in the ball park," Leonard said, "but maybe under the bleachers somewhere."

"I was reaching for something there."

"And didn't quite get it," Leonard said.

"You like those vanilla cookies I keep here?" Brett said.

"You are wise, and you have great ways of using old clichés," Leonard said.

"Like when you said thick as thieves?" Brett said.

"Just like that."

Chance laughed. It was soft and short and throaty, and that made me smile. "Come on, Dad," she said. "Give me an example of your dad's wisdom."

"Alright. I can tell you an incident that shows that, and his sense of justice."

I was twelve then, and the country was not like it is now. There were still plenty of tall and ancient hardwoods on either side of the road, mixed with pines and sweet gums and all manner of other trees, and the squirrels were thick in the hardwoods, and the birds when nested in them were so many they looked like colorful blooms.

Daddy drove up a hill in our old black car, and at the top of the hill we coasted down a ways, and then turned left onto a red clay road so narrow the limbs of trees brushed lightly against the windows and whispered over the hood and the roof of the car. It was a cool early winter day and the trees cast shadows across the little road we were on.

After a while, we turned off, and ended up at the end of a sandy rutted road even more narrow than the clay one. There was a car parked there, right next to the woods. A white Chevrolet. Daddy parked next to it, and we got out. Daddy pulled two shotguns from the back seat, a twelve gauge for him, and a four/ten for me.

Both guns were single shot and broken open and unloaded, and Daddy left them that way. He handed me the four/ten, placed his shotgun on the hood of our car, and looked at the Chevy as he pulled on a red vest that had our ammunition in it and some jerky he had brought.

"Hank Jenner's car," he said.

I knew Hank Jenner only faintly. He was a burly guy with tobacco-stained teeth and he wore a greasy fedora, the brim of which was turned down to canopy his eyes. He spent a lot of time at the feed store talking to other men who, like him, seemed to have little to do. I would see him when I went to buy comic books next door, and when I came by the open doorway of the feed store, walking along the sidewalk, he always said something or another. I never understood exactly what it was he was getting at, and he said things to my mother too, leaning out of the doorway to do it, but she ignored him. The men in the store laughed.

One time she told me, "Don't say anything about Mr. Jenner to your Daddy, about anything he said."

"Why?"

"Because if you do, Mrs. Jenner, who is a very nice lady, will be sleeping alone."

I didn't understand that exactly, not then. I did know Mama and Daddy didn't like Mr. Jenner. Other than his crowd down at the feed store, not many did. No one could figure out what he did for a living, but he always had a bit of money. Most of it went for chewing tobacco, and according to Daddy, lots of alcohol.

I liked Mr. Jenner's wife. She was my fourth grade teacher. She was sweet and funny and had kids of her own, some younger, some older than me. None were in my classes.

If I saw her out of school, with her husband, she seemed different. Not as tall as in the classroom, never smiling, and she never stopped to talk to anyone. She never wore one of the three or four nice dresses she wore to class, but instead old, gray things. Her kids were dressed poorly as well. At school they had a few good clothes, but away from there they wore old stuff. I understood that. My mother sewed my clothes mostly, and there were hand-me-downs from my cousins that I wore as they outgrew them. When I wasn't at school, or being made to go to church, I wore older clothes with patched knees and elbows. This was, and still is, a poor part of the country.

Sometimes Mr. Jenner would be waiting on Mrs. Jenner when school was over. He would park at the curb, get out and cross his arms, lean on his car, and wait for her to come out. You could see her grow smaller as she walked toward the car. They never spoke. She just got in.

On this hunting day I was excited, and the sight of Mr. Jenner's car meant little to me. A lot of people hunted those woods. I suppose the property belonged to somebody, but back then there was an understood rule that you could hunt on other people's property as long as you didn't shoot everything in sight, cut fences, or build unattended fires. I liked to shoot squirrels, and had gone hunting several times, and we had eaten what I killed like Daddy said we had to do. If we didn't kill anything, I knew we'd be having cornmeal mush for dinner.

We went into the woods along an animal path, doing what was called "still" hunting. We didn't have a hunting dog, we just walked and looked up and watched for a squirrel's tail to blow in the wind, and then we shot it. We had a strict number of squirrels we killed, and then two more for a poor colored family. That was what African-Americans were called then. Colored.

They lived not far from us. The man of the house had a bad foot injury and could only do light work, so they always needed food and money. His wife did cleaning and the children worked part-time jobs and went to the colored school beyond Marvel Creek at a place called Sand Ridge. A lot of coloreds lived there.

I existed in a state of confusion because Daddy cussed "the niggers and the burr-heads and the jigs," but was always giving them extra squirrels he shot, or extra fish he caught. When we didn't catch many fish or killed only a few squirrels, he would give them all away, and corn meal mush would be in the offing.

Yet, at home, way he talked about colored people in general was pretty tough and made me kind of sick to my stomach, even though I wasn't exactly sure why.

Mama saw the good in people, no matter their color.

She and Daddy talked very different about the colored folks, though they both seemed kind and generous with everyone, and Daddy, oddly, considering how he talked, seemed even more that way with the colored. The best I ever came to understanding him, was when he once said he knew what it was like to be hungry.

Out in the woods, carrying our shotguns, me and Daddy walked along for a while. It was fall and the oaks had shed their leaves. The pines were eternally green unless dying. The air smelled of trees and dirt and nearby water from the Sabine River.

After a bit, I saw a squirrel and Daddy let me shoot him. It was a good shot, and the squirrel fell. I grabbed it by the tail and tied it off to my belt with a piece of twine, and we carried on.

It was about midday when we stopped to eat something. I had killed two squirrels and Daddy had killed two. Daddy pulled out the jerky inside his vest, unwrapped the wax paper it was in, and gave me a piece.

"Eat slow, we might be a while before supper," Daddy said.

I chewed slowly, pretending I was Davy Crockett on a hunt for bears.

Daddy said, "You like shooting those squirrels, don't you?"

"Yes, sir."

"Well, them squirrels are food. Okay to be glad about food, but you start shooting to watch something fall, start thinking killing is good, you need to sit down on a log like this and have a little talk with yourself. Killing ain't no good thing, son, unless it's to eat or protect yourself. And you ought never to delight in it."

That's how Daddy was. He said things kind of off to the side sometimes, and then you'd think on it and understand it. But I certainly had been delighting in killing those squirrels. Guns and killing made you feel powerful.

When we finished eating, hunting continued, and we killed one more a piece. We were about to start back to the car, when Daddy saw something bright red on the ground between some sycamore trees, and there was something black on the red and it moved and shimmered in the strips of sunlight that fell between the boughs of the trees. We went over to it.

Daddy took me by the shoulders and told me to go stand by a big elm he pointed at, and I did. I could see what was lying on the ground, though, and I had seen it close up. A man with most of his head missing. I had shot a squirrel earlier and most of its head was gone, but I hadn't felt the same way then. Flies had risen up in a cloud when we came upon the body, and now the cloud was descending again. The body was soon covered in them, and when they moved it was in mass, as if they were all part of one kind of creature. You could see bits of his red shirt between the mass of flies, and then for some reason or another, they would rise up in a blast and then come down again. The air smelled sour.

Something, a wild dog or coyote or red wolf, perhaps, had pulled off one of the body's cowboy boots which lay nearby, and had gnawed at a socked foot. It didn't even look like a foot anymore, and most of the sock was missing and part of it had been pulled out in a long strand. A greasy fedora lay nearby, on its crown, and by the body was a rifle.

"Jenner," Dad said.

You couldn't tell that by the face, but we knew it was him, way he was dressed, shape of his body, his car being parked at the edge of the woods.

Daddy leaned over the body and gave it a closer look. He glanced at Jenner's thirty/thirty on the ground beside him. He stood up and walked around Jenner and bent down and looked at the leafy ground. He ran his finger into something in the dirt. I couldn't help myself. I moved away from the elm just enough to see it was a footprint, and there were others. They were small footprints and they led off toward the river, which at that point you could hear it gurgling along not far from us.

Even at that age, it came to me those prints were out of place. Jenner was a big man with big feet. Those prints were much smaller and had been made the day before. I knew that, because they were dried now, and they had been impacted in the earth when it was wet. It had rained yesterday.

Daddy came over and pulled a big pack of chewing

tobacco out of his pocket and stuck a wad in his cheek. He didn't say anything, just cradled his shotgun in his arms.

"We gonna tell the sheriff?" I said.

"In good time. He ain't gonna get no deader."

We started back for the car. It took about an hour to make our way out of the woods. Dad stopped by the Chevy, and did a curious thing. He took a handkerchief out of his pocket and used it to open the front passenger-side door. He stuck his head inside, and then he picked up a black purse off the front seat, shoved the door shut with his knee.

"Get in the car, Baby Man."

I opened the back door to our car and snapped open my shotgun. The shell had already been fired, and it popped out and onto the ground. I picked it up and put it in my pocket with the other empties, and placed the four/ten on the backseat. I got in the car, and Dad placed his shotgun on the back seat as well, and dropped the purse onto the front seat.

When he was sitting behind the wheel, I said, "What happened to Mr. Jenner?"

"I'm going to say an accident."

"We telling the sheriff?"

I had already asked this, but it was on my mind. I had seen a lot of TV shows and movies, and something like this happened, you told the sheriff, the cops, the law.

"Shortly," he said.

I looked down at the purse. It looked familiar.

After driving out of the woods, when we turned off onto the main road we didn't go toward our house. We went the other way.

"Where we going, Daddy?"

"Little thing to do," he said.

I guess we drove for about twenty minutes or so before we came to a house set off the road. It was at the back of about an acre of property. Great trees grew in the front yard, and the grass was dead as most grass was dead that time of year; it had turned brown as toast. The house was big, but it was old too, one of those that had a porch around it and a dog run right through the middle. The paint was peeling off the house in strips that reminded me of the way skin peels off of you when you've had a sunburn and it's a few days after. There was woods behind the house, and I realized the river was close as well. As the crow flew, where we had found Mr. Jenner was a short distance from the back of the Jenner house, much closer than by car.

"You sit right here, alright?" Daddy said.

"Yes, sir."

He took the purse and got out of the car.

Even though it was winter, it wasn't cold, just cool. I had my window rolled down, and I rested my elbow on the window frame and thought about the body in the woods, but I didn't think on it long. I don't know if it was because I disliked Mr. Jenner, or because my mind didn't want to keep thinking on that, his head blown off and the rising and lowering of that cloud of flies.

Instead, after a few moments I thought of supper. I was starting to think about fried squirrel. I hoped Mama had pulled some dandelion greens or some such to go with it. First though, when we got home, I had to skin and clean the squirrels. That was my job. To skin them by cutting the fur loose at the back legs near the feet, peeling it back from there, and pulling it over the squirrel's head, like a night shirt. Then I would cut the head off and gut the squirrel, careful not to drag my knife through the squirrel's ass first, but instead I would cut down from its stomach to the ass, pull out the guts for the dog. I would hose the squirrel off then, wash out its empty belly, and give it to Mama to cut up and cook.

That was what was on my mind while I sat there, but those thoughts went away when Mrs. Jenner appeared. She opened the door and stood at the screen for a moment, then pushed the screen door open and came out. She closed the screen gently behind her, crossed the porch and came down the steps. This took her a long while to do. She had on a very old dress, so faded it was nearly white, and if the sun had been bright, you could have seen through it. Mrs. Jenner's skin was almost as pale as her dress, and sunlight might not only have shown through the dress, it occurred to me that it might even show through her, though there was one dark spot on her: her left eye was black and swollen. It was then that Mr. Jenner's image came back to me, that blown-away head and the hard, dried blood spread out on the ground like paint. Something was churning around in my young head, but I couldn't quite get hold of what it was.

Daddy handed Mrs. Jenner the purse. I could hear him clearly.

"Found this."

"Oh," she said, and took it.

She stood looking at Daddy, as if she wasn't sure if he was really there or not. I thought she didn't seem sure she was there. At the front door one of the kids looked out through the screen, and then went back inside.

"Your husband," I heard Daddy say, "I found him in the woods where we hunt."

"Oh," she said.

"He's dead."

"Is he?"

It was as if she had been told he had a flat tire and would be home late.

"He was shot with a shotgun."

"I see," she said.

"Could be a hunting accident. Tripped on a limb, the gun went off and killed him. It happens."

"It does, doesn't it?" She crossed her arms and put her elbows in her palms.

"But only a thirty/thirty was on the ground. I think since he was shot with a shotgun, he should have had a shotgun there. He's not far back there behind the house. His car is parked off the road."

"Yeah, he never liked crossing the rickety old river bridge."

"It's not a good bridge for a big man to test," Daddy said. "But someone smaller, and lighter, it would be a good way to go."

She nodded. "He made me go hunting with him sometimes."

It was Daddy's turn to nod.

"I didn't really like it, but he made me go."

Daddy nodded again.

"I think he's been there a day, and I'm going to report it. But it will take me time to go to town, because I drive pretty slow."

She studied Daddy's face.

"I think since he was shot with a shotgun, that's what should be there. It's hard to explain that thirty/thirty, but I may have looked at it wrong. It might have been a shotgun lying there. It sure could be. It ought to be, you know, considering what happened. The accident and all."

"Of course."

"Sorry to bring the bad news."

"No problem," she said. "Someone had to tell me."

"Lucky we came across him, so you'd know."

"Yeah. It is."

"We're going to go now, and I'm sorry about your husband."

"You said you were going to tell the sheriff."

"I am, but like I said, I drive slow, and I may stop off at the store to buy some milk and bread. Yeah. I'm going to do that first, then I'm going to tell the sheriff. It might take a while."

"Please do take your time," she said.

Daddy nodded at her. "I'll go then."

Daddy climbed into the car and started the engine, but he didn't put the car in gear. He just sat there. We sat there for a while.

I said, "Daddy, what are you doing?"

"Sitting on a log."

"What?"

"Having a talk with myself."

"Sir?"

"It's alright, son."

Dad put the car in reverse and backed around, put it in drive, and drove us out of there. I looked back and saw that Mrs. Jenner had come out the back door and was crossing the backyard. She was wearing men's pants and had on boots and was carrying something, but we had reached the edge of the woods along the road near her house, and I only got a glimpse of her, and then I couldn't see her anymore.

When we were on the road, Daddy said, "What kind of gun did you see lying by Mr. Jenner?"

"A rifle," I said.

"No, son. It was a shotgun. Anyone asks you, it was a shotgun. I thought it was a thirty/thirty too, but it wasn't."

I knew what I had seen, but in that moment, I understood, or at least understood enough.

"Yes, sir," I said. "A shotgun."

Mrs. Jenner taught the rest of the semester, and she dressed well all the time and smiled outside of class, and then when the semester ended, she and her children moved off and I never saw or heard of her again.

14.
THE OAK AND THE POND

When I finished with the story, Chance said, "I love that. Can you tell me more?"

I saw Brett glance at the clock.

"Nope, not tonight," I said. "I have to take Uncle Leonard home."

"He could sleep on the couch," Chance said. "We could stay up awhile, like a slumber party."

"Nope," Leonard said, "it's been a long day and a hard workout, time for me to go to my place and crash."

"Dang it," Chance said.

"Next time we do pizza, sit and tell stories," I said.

"Promise?" Chance said. She seemed so much like a little girl then, and I guess, when you get older, someone in their twenties, even thirties, seems like a kid to you.

"Promise," I said.

I drove Leonard home, and on the way he nodded off. When I stopped at his place he came wide awake. "Damn, you could have just drove around with me in the car and let me sleep."

"That's how they do babies," I said. "You are not a baby."

"I might be someone's baby."

"Not mine, though."

Leonard reached out and tapped me on the shoulder with his fist. "Tomorrow, bro."

"You bet."

He got out and I drove off. Thing was, though, I wasn't that tired. All the talk had made me nostalgic. I drove out to where Leonard used to live, where Trudy died and other bad things happened. There were good memories there too, and I tried to concentrate on those. I drove out here now and again, sometimes with Leonard, and each time I told myself I wouldn't do it again, but I did. It was like an alcoholic that says he won't take another drink, then goes to the cabinet immediately after the thought and pulls down the bottle.

But it wasn't Trudy I was thinking about now, not really, it was the place where Leonard had lived and the woods behind it and the Robin Hood tree.

At one time there was a great oak tree behind the house where Leonard was living then, and the oak was deep in the woods, and it was one of the last of the great oaks. It stood tall and thick and ancient. It had great limbs you could crawl up on and stretch out on and sleep without real fear of rolling off.

We called it the Robin Hood tree, like the great tree where Robin and his merry band of men gathered to talk and feast. I also thought of it as the Tarzan tree, imagined how you could build a treehouse on its massive limbs and have plenty of room to live with a lithe, blonde Jane and do more than call elephants and swing on vines.

Leonard and I would meet at the oak, me having hiked through the woods from my place. My place wasn't all that far if you came by wooded path, then broke off the path and took a deer trail, and finally a winding trace through a series of tall blackjack oaks until you arrived at Fisherman's Creek. Across the creek the trees thinned in number but not in magnificence. There were sweet gums and hickory trees, and of course pines.

The Robin Hood tree was the granddaddy of them all. The oak rose higher and spread its limbs wider than all the others. Its bark was healthy and dark, and in the spring its leaves were green as Ireland. To stand beneath it when it rained was a miracle, because the limbs were so thick and the leaves so plush that during the spring, and much of the summer, if not the fall when the leaves were brown and yellow and falling, you would hardly get wet. When it stormed the limbs shook like angry soldiers rattling their weapons, but the limbs didn't break, just old dead leaves and little branches dribbled down. The soil beneath the oak was thick and dark with many years of dropped and composted leaves. There were acorns on the ground, and sometimes when you came to the tree, squirrels were beneath it, rare black squirrels that made this part of the woods their home. They were in the tree too, chattering and fussing as you arrived.

Leonard and I met there many mornings, usually having a breakfast of boiled eggs we had brought in sacks, drinking coffee from our thermoses, carrying fishing gear and small coolers with our lunches in them.

We would sometimes sit there beneath the tree and talk, and finally we would go away from there, carrying our coolers, through the trees, and then along the creek line to where the pond was. It was a big pond, and at one point in time there had been a house near it. Now the house was a pile of gray lumber and rusty nails and a few bricks that showed where the fireplace had been. Beyond that was a clapboard barn that still stood, the great wide doors gone, probably taken for lumber for someone's project. Trees crowded it, and one sweet gum had grown up and under the roof and was pushing it loose on one side.

The pond had been dug maybe fifty years before and had been filled with fish, and we were fishing their descendants. There was a boat down there, one we had tediously carried there along the creek bank, and we left it for when we wanted to fish. No one bothered it, because no one came there anymore but us. The land was owned by someone up north who had mostly forgotten about it. The pond was always muddy, but the fish were thick. We caught them and generally threw them back, unless they were good-sized enough and fat. Then they went home with us and became our supper.

We fished there with cane poles, not rods and reels. It wasn't a place for rods and reels. It was a place for fishing in an old and simple way. We put lines on the poles, sinkers, corks, hooks, and bait, usually worms. Out in the boat we would dangle lines and watch the fish jump, the dragonflies dip down on the water, see the shadows of birds flying over, now and again there was the sight of a leaping frog or a wiggling water moccasin. Turtle heads rose like periscopes, then fell beneath the water with a delicate splash and a small ripple.

In the spring it was cool for a long time, and in the summer it grew hot, but with wide-brimmed hats on, we still fished, and we lazed, and sometimes we talked, softly, fearing we might frighten the fish. We talked about all manner of things we believed in, and how we differed from one another. I told Leonard about my women, and he told me about his men. We talked about brotherhood without speaking of it directly. I told bad jokes and Leonard grumbled.

When Leonard moved from the house next to the woods, and I later moved from where I lived, we lost that spot.

Some years later the people up north remembered the land, and they brought in pulp crews and cut the woods down, even the great and ancient oak, which must have fought the saws with its old, hard wood. But the saws won, and it tumbled down and was coated in gasoline and set on fire. They didn't even bother to make it into lumber. The land where it stood was a black spot for a long time.

They planted rows and rows of soft lumber pines to be cut and replanted every fifteen or twenty years, a crop. People claim there are more trees now than before, but they are wrong. Once you could drive all through East Texas and there were trees as far as you could see, and not just pines either. The trees grew close to the roads and covered them in shadow. You don't have to go out in the woods and count trees one by one to know that the statements being made about there being more trees than ever before is a bald-faced lie. The pines they planted where the oak grew didn't shield you from rain or rattle in the wind the way the Robin Hood tree did.

Eventually, they filled in the pond, killing the fish. They dammed up the creek and made another, larger pond farther up, but it lacked charm, and finally scummed over. Nothing lived in it.

A company that raised chickens for a supermarket chain bought the land, and a series of long, commercial chicken houses took the place of the original pond and the woods that had surrounded it, even the pulp trees, which they also cut down and didn't replant. Now there is a wide gravel road that leads out of where the trees once grew, on to the highway. It's odd. Looking down that gravel road, you can see the highway so easy. It seemed farther away in the years before the road was there and the trees were cut.

Leonard wouldn't even look in the direction of the

old place when we drove by. I look, but I don't like what I see. The rain still falls and the wind still blows, but the oak and the pond are gone.

AFTERWORD

So I bring you something different.

The Mosaic Novel. I didn't invent that term. I don't know who did, but the idea is that it's a novel that is not in order of the events, nor are all the events designed to roll precisely into the other. It is like a notebook where someone has been randomly recording events of their life and it's been found by a passerby. Some pages might even be missing, but the stories, in order, or out of order, constitute a portion of a young man's life.

The early life of one Hap Collins.

Leonard Pine, his close friend, and eventually his brother, appears as well. I know what this is like, to make your own family. I have a good family by blood, thank goodness, but I have some true brothers and sisters out there, like Andrew Vachss for example. Nick Damici. We just know, and there's no other way to explain it.

When I was growing up it was not unusual for there to be books connected loosely by this sort of tissue, and for the stories to gradually give you an overall view of a character's life, or a thematic overview of a town, or even something science fictional, like Ray Bradbury's version of Mars in *The Martian Chronicles*, or something far more earthbound as in Hemingway's *Nick Adams Stories*.

Those are merely two examples of many books of that nature. This is a modern example of that. I love the stories here. They are not all heroic or adventurous, but they do fill in a lot of reader gaps. Here you get some background you might not have gotten from the books. Most of it about Hap. Leonard is not in all the stories, and not all the stories are about Hap, even if he narrates. There is even a third person approach to some of the material. It felt right.

Hap and Leonard have become brothers by the time my first novel in the series, *Savage Season*, occurs, but before that they were two guys feeling out a friendship, finding it good, but it was not quite at the level of what it would eventually be. They would become family.

I love these guys. They have been with me a long time. I have had a lot of time to visit with them, and lately more than usual. New books, new novellas, a TV show, and now these stories. Some of them are brand new, some of them are rare, and only a couple have had much life outside of small presentations. "The Boy Who Became Invisible" appeared in a previous collection from the same publisher, but somehow it would have left too big a gap in this series of events had we restricted its presence merely because it appeared before. Here it becomes a valuable part of this mosaic construction. Same with "Not Our Kind," though it has only appeared in the aforementioned book, which by the way is titled *Hap and Leonard*.

I am proud of these stories. I am proud of Hap and Leonard. They may even have broken a bit of new ground in their day. I won't go into all of that, as I have written about their odd couple differences before.

I am also proud of Hap and Leonard's influence on other writers, and I am happy to have those writers write and tell me how much the books meant to them, and how much they helped them create their own characters. And all you readers, Hap and Leonard fans, thank you.

As a side note, these stories may in fact violate some of the material in the novels, but not by much. These are the true stories, the true past. In the novels Hap dropped a step now and then, not revealing things, hinting at things, and in a couple of small cases he was just wrong. The TV show, soon to go into its second season, has borrowed some of the ideas in some of these stories, some true events from my life, and they have given Hap and Leonard a slightly different past than the one here, but as they say in the movie business, it is "in the spirit of," which generally means bend over, no time to grease up, here it comes. But in my case I have been treated very well by the series, and so have my characters. I appreciate that. Thanks SundanceTV for not screwing it up. Still, there are differences in the TV version and my version. The record is set straight here. This is the official version.

Enjoy your visit with Hap and Leonard in the early days. I certainly enjoyed finding out about them myself. Hap has not always been as open with me about his past as I would have liked.

Joe R. Lansdale
Nacogdoches, Texas
2016

ABOUT THE AUTHOR

Joe R. Lansdale is the author of more than forty novels and four hundred shorter works, including stories, essays, introductions, and articles. He has written screenplays and teleplays, including for *Batman: The Animated Series* and *Superman: The Animated Series*. He wrote the script for the animated film *The Son of Batman*. His works have been translated into numerous languages, and several novels and short stories of his have been filmed, among them *Bubba Ho-Tep*; *Cold in July*; *Incident On and Off a Mountain Road*, for Showtime's *Masters of Horror*; and *Christmas with the Dead*, which he produced with a screenplay by his son, Keith.

Lansdale is the recipient of numerous awards and recognitions, among them the Edgar Award and ten Bram Stoker Awards, one of which is for Lifetime Achievement. He has received the Grandmaster of Horror Award; the

British Fantasy Award; the Inkpot Award for Lifetime Achievement; the Herodotus Award for historical/crime fiction; the Golden Lion Award for his contribution to the works of Edgar Rice Burroughs; the Grinzane Prize; and others.

Lansdale is also a member of the Texas Literary Hall of Fame and the Texas Institute of Letters, and he is Writer in Residence at Stephen F. Austin State University. He is the founder of Shen Chuan Martial Science and has been recognized by the International Martial Arts Hall of Fame as well as the United States Martial Arts Hall of Fame.

Joe Lansdale lives with his wife, Karen, in Nacogdoches, Texas.